THE BROODING LAKE

In 1890, Abbey Sinclair begins work as companion to Henrietta Kershaw at Kerslake Hall in Yorkshire. Abbey becomes attracted to both Mrs Kershaw's son Antony, and her nephew Thomas Craddock. She also befriends Alice, governess to Antony's daughter Emily. But many secrets lurk at Kerslake Hall. Who screams in the tower in the dead of night, and how did two women die in the brooding lake? Attempting to discover answers to these questions, Abbey is in danger of losing not only her heart, but her life too . . .

ROSEMARY A. SMITH

◆

THE BROODING LAKE

Complete and Unabridged

LINFORD
Leicester

First published in Great Britain in 2006

First Linford Edition
published 2007

British Library CIP Data

Smith, Rosemary A.
    The brooding lake.—Large print ed.—
Linford romance library
    1. Yorkshire (England)—Fiction
    2. Love stories 3. Large type books
    I. Title
    823.9'2 [F]

    ISBN 978–1–84617–645–6

Published by
F. A. Thorpe (Publishing) F
Anstey, Leicestershire

Set by Words & Graphics Ltd.
Anstey, Leicestershire
Printed and bound in Great Britain by
T. J. International Ltd., Padstow, Cornwall

This book is printed on acid-free paper

Dedicated with love
to the memory of my friend
Beryl Lord of East Budleigh
who appreciated the written word,
and was a wonderful conversationalist.
You are greatly missed.

1

I stood in the hot July sun watching the coach and horses which had conveyed me from York trundle away in the distance across the Yorkshire moors. I looked at the signpost which pointed to Kerslake Hall and then surveyed the small trunk and valise at my feet. There was little chance that I could carry them the two miles indicated to the Hall.

My brow was hot and I brushed my equally warm hand across it with little relief, it was tempting to remove my straw boater and mauve short wide-collared jacket, but knew it would not be seemly even in this wilderness, for that is how it appeared to me.

The track I would need to traverse was rough and uneven, no trees were in sight where I could have rested for a while in the shade. The high-necked collar of my white blouse was suffocating and swiftly I loosened the large bow, undoing the top button, now I could at least breathe.

While mulling over what to do it would seem help was moving towards me in the form of a brown pony and small trap. As the young man came to a halt on the dusty road beside me he raised his cap.

'Can I help you, Miss?' he asked in a pleasant Yorkshire brogue while glancing at my luggage.

'I am bound for Kerslake Hall,' I replied with hope, although knowing it would be unconventional to accept assistance from this stranger, but it appeared I had no other choice and he seemed pleasant enough. The young man looked over my head into the distance somehow deliberating what to do.

'There's not many that would venture near the Hall since . . . ' His words trailed away.

'Since what?' I enquired somewhat

sharply, was it with anxiety or impatience I wondered.

'Not for me to say, Miss, but I can see the predicament you are in, let me help you on board.' So saying he jumped down, swiftly storing my luggage in the back of the trap, and then assisting me on to the seat beside him, my flared petticoats almost sticking to my legs.

We moved slowly along the uneven track, out of the corner of my eye I could see him glancing at me from time to time. I kept silent until he spoke.

'My name's Harry,' he said, 'And yours, Miss?'

At this question I was reticent to offer a name but in view of his help realised it would be rude not to. 'Abbey Sinclair,' I offered quietly.

'A lovely name if I may be so bold, Miss, and quite appropriate as there are many abbeys in these parts albeit they are ruined.' That piece of information was pleasing to my ear as I had a love of history which prompted my next question.

'Is there one near the Hall?' I asked with interest.

'There most certainly is Miss, not far from the surrounding wall. I don't know for sure, but would imagine you could see Thurston Abbey from an upper window.'

The ground was flat, covered with a springy carpet of beautiful purple heather. On the horizon there were ranges of hills some higher than others, the tops of which were obscured by a heat haze, then ahead of me on the right I caught sight of a large grey forbidding-looking building surrounded by a high granite wall. Harry must have heard my sharp intake of breath.

'Still time to change your mind Miss, for that is indeed Kerslake Hall.'

At his words I was sorely tempted to instruct Harry to retrace our journey, but then I thought of Mrs Henrietta Kershaw who would be expecting me, and maybe it wouldn't be so bad as it appeared, but then if the place looked so eerie in sunlight, what would it look like in the dead of winter?

'Please stop for a moment, Harry, for I need to collect my thoughts.' Without realising it, as I spoke I gently touched his arm as he drew Bessie to a halt. What am I doing here? I asked myself already knowing the answer, in this year of Our Lord 1890 an impoverished young woman had but two courses to follow in life, marriage or a position as governess or companion.

As I was twenty-five years of age the former had obviously eluded me, so the latter had been inevitable and I had found myself being interviewed by a starchy solicitor named Mr Lang for position of companion to a Mrs Kershaw of Kerslake Hall in Yorkshire.

It had all seemed very romantic sat in Mr Lang's office, but now it would seem somewhat unfortunate that I had been successful in securing the post. I would however endure it for a short time, after all Mrs Kershaw may be a very amenable person, unlike the exterior of her home. Little did I know then, thankfully, what sort of person she would turn out to be.

Harry set me down outside the iron gates which were flanked either side by pillars, on top of which sat two demons with open mouths and fiery tongues. He graciously excused himself from helping me with my luggage and with little ado was gone leaving me stood in a blast of dust due to the speed of his departure.

Tentatively I pressed down the iron latch and the gate swung open with ease, squealing as it came to a halt against the hedge, which lined the drive on either side. Picking up my luggage I hesitated before stepping across the boundary of the Hall. I placed the luggage down once more before closing the gate, retying the bow on my blouse I picked up trunk and valise and proceeded up the long path.

Everywhere was silent and I had a fancy that the place was in truth uninhabited, when a large black raven swooped noisily over the top of my head almost dislodging my hat, so close had it flown, leaving me trembling and somewhat startled.

The house loomed up on me suddenly as I looked at the tall three storey building with many large plain glass windows I had an overwhelming feeling of familiarity, yet I was sure I'd never been here before in my life.

At the far end of the building on the left was a small round turreted tower, although attached to the house it looked incongruous and somehow filled me with dread. I had had my chance to retreat but it was too late for as I looked, the double front doors opened as if by themselves, before a tall woman appeared in the doorway at the top of the steps.

'I take it you are Miss Sinclair?' she called out to me in a cultured voice.

'I am indeed,' I answered moving towards the bottom of the steps, my feet crunching on the gravel beneath.

'Mrs Kershaw is expecting you, indeed waiting for you,' she added, almost as an afterthought. As she spoke I looked at my fob watch and realised that I was one-and-a-half hours late, not a good start, but I didn't really care as my intention was to leave this cold gloomy house at the first opportunity.

As I stepped across the threshold the woman who bade me enter closed the doors behind me, I could barely see the huge hall I had stepped into for the sun did not reach this side of the house at this time of day. All I could ascertain were shadowy corners and a musty smell, as though the house were unlived in.

'I'm Mrs Grafton.' Her voice brought me back to the present, 'I'd like to welcome you to Kerslake Hall and ask that in future you use the servants' entrance.'

'Which is where?' I interrupted sharply, for I felt anything but welcome in this gloomy place.

'At the far side of the house,

someone will show you later,' replied Mrs Grafton through gritted teeth, she was obviously unused to being questioned. 'Please leave your bags here, as before I show you your room, Mrs Kershaw wishes to speak with you, follow me!'

Doing as I was bid, I followed the slim, grey-clad woman to the back of the hall and along a corridor which was sparsely carpeted in green, my eyes were adjusting to the light and I could see many small pieces of furniture set against the purple-coloured wallpaper. Mrs Grafton opened a large wooden door, and as she did I was blinded by sunlight which streamed through one of the large windows on the left.

'Miss Sinclair has arrived, Mistress.' Seconds after she spoke I heard Mrs Grafton close the door behind her, I could hardly see the room let alone my employer, so blinded was I by the light.

'You're late.' A harsh voice admonished me with two simple words.

I stepped forward out of the sunlight

and looked in the direction from which the voice came.

'Have you lost your tongue girl?'

As I looked at the owner of the voice I could scarcely believe my eyes. A small female form was sitting in an armchair by a large granite fireplace, she was dressed in brown which matched the brown leather chair she sat in, her feet resting on a stool with an ebony stick leaning against her chair.

What fascinated me more than anything was the fact that a black spotted veil covered her face, I could just see her grey hair and pallid face through the fine mesh and quite garishly, the bright red rouge she wore on her thin lips.

I disliked her instantly from her harsh voice to the bony hands which lay on her lap. 'Don't stare girl, I'm not a spectacle at some circus. So Abbey Sinclair, you are to be my paid companion.' Her voice stressed the word paid, which caused me to dislike her even further as she continued. 'My guess is you are really named Abigail, come on girl speak, I'm right, aren't I?'

'Yes,' I managed to utter trying desperately to keep control of my rising temper.

'I thought as much, well that's what I shall call you for I don't hold with pet names, we should all use the names that we were given. Your job will not be difficult as I don't need much company, I prefer my own, but my eyesight is failing and I need someone to read to me. I take it you can read, girl?'

'Yes,' I replied ungraciously, for her manner was irking me.

'Thank the Lord for that at least. Your clothes do not please me, far too gaudy, have you anything grey?' As she spoke I looked down at the mauve suit I had painstakingly saved for to make a good impression. The flared skirt fell beautifully across the toes of my black ankle boots and the jacket to match with leg of mutton sleeves was plain except for some piping on the wide lapels, the whole outfit I felt was quite reserved and appropriate. How dare she? I was very much my own person and resented being dictated to as to what I should wear.

'I ask again, have you anything grey?' the voice reiterated.

'Yes,' I answered, quite resolved to leave this place as soon as I left this woman's presence.

There was a sudden commotion behind me as the door opened to reveal a pretty dark-haired girl aged about ten years, dressed in a pretty powder blue dress with white stockings and black shiny shoes.

'Grandmamma,' she shouted running across to Mrs Kershaw who put out a bony hand to take the child's offered one.

'Miss Hayward, how many times have I asked you not to let Emily burst into my room unannounced?' As she spoke I turned to look at the recipient of Mrs Kershaw's displeasure.

A tall serene-looking young woman with pale brown hair stood by the door, her hands clasped in front of her. She was dressed in a dove grey dress which fitted in at her small waist, flimsy grey frills fell from the neck not quite concealing her slender white throat. She was a lovely creature.

The child gave life to the drab room which was sparsely furnished with just a large table and two huge brown leather armchairs. In contrast bright yellow curtains hung at the windows.

'I'm sorry Mrs Kershaw, but the child was longing to see you and I could not keep up with her as she ran down the stairs and along the corridor.'

I listened to Miss Hayward's soft almost reverent voice and wondered how she kept so calm at Mrs Kershaw's manner towards her; I could not be so subservient.

'This is Abigail Sinclair, newly arrived, Miss Hayward, and this is my over zealous granddaughter, Emily.' As she spoke I looked from one to the other, Emily was by now sat at Mrs Kershaw's feet stroking a long-haired white cat that I had not noticed before. The child's governess stood demurely by the door looking down at the floor, she seemed not to want to meet my eye or talk to me, maybe this would alter out of the old lady's domineering presence.

'I'm weary.' Mrs Kershaw's voice drifted across to me, although weary her voice was still harsh and hostile.

'Please, Miss Hayward show Abigail to the hall and take Emily for her tea. Goodbye, pet, I'll see you tomorrow.' As she ruffled her granddaughter's hair her voice was gentle each time she addressed the child. 'No Emily, you can't take Charles with you, put him down.'

Emily put the purring cat back in his bed at the old lady's feet and ran to take Miss Hayward's hand. I followed them out realising that I'd uttered only three words since entering the room and summed up that the old lady had an acid tongue.

I was pleased to follow Miss Hayward, as stepping back into the corridor it was dark and shadowy once more. Emily skipped along quite unperturbed at the darkness, the silent Miss Hayward walked ahead of me her back straight and head held high.

As we reached the entrance hall once more the front door opened and a man stood silhouetted in the doorway. 'Father! Father!' Emily exclaimed, releasing the grip of Miss Hayward's hand she ran to him and he gathered her in his arms in a strong embrace, this child was obviously well loved.

As he stepped farther into the hallway I could see he was a tall slim man of about thirty-five years of age, the sun had bleached his already blond hair and I could see as he turned his attention to me that his eyes were a startling blue.

'You must be Miss Sinclair.' As he spoke he gently removed his daughter from him. 'I'm Antony Kershaw,

15

welcome to my home, I trust you will be happy here.' He offered his hand to me which I took gladly, this was a genuine welcome indeed. So the abominable Mrs Kershaw was not the mistress here and I smiled. Almost reading my thoughts he continued.

'Have you met my mother?'

'I have indeed, not a moment since,' I replied with feeling.

'And what did you make of her?' he asked politely.

'She is somewhat daunting and also very rude,' I said honestly. A brief smile hovered on Antony Kershaw's lips.

'You sum her up very well, Miss Sinclair, but I assure you her bark is worse than her bite, just give her a chance. Since my wife,' here he hesitated momentarily, 'since my wife died two years ago, things have not been easy for any of us. The last two companions employed for my mother have left within days. I trust this will not be the case with you.'

His words were a challenge and

shortly afterwards as I followed Mrs Grafton up the stone staircase to my room, my mind was in a whirl. I'd sensed hostility at every turn in the brief time I'd been in the house, except from Mr Kershaw and his child Emily, even the lovely Miss Hayward had not spoken, but watched me with a silent, unfathomable manner.

I wondered also why my employer covered her face with a veil, and did everyone in the house apart from Emily and the old lady wear grey? For Antony Kershaw also wore it in the form of a country suit, and the hat he had removed was of grey felt with a curled brim. I had quite taken to the man and felt in some way sorry for the position he was in with a domineering mother and a young daughter to contend with.

2

My room was small and adequate, the polished wooden floorboards were covered by a small beige-coloured rug, there was a single wardrobe in one corner adjacent to the door with a matching dressing table next to it. The window opposite cast light onto the bevelled mirror.

Mrs Grafton left me to settle in, telling me that I could either eat in my room or share the table in the kitchen with the rest of the household staff.

Before arranging my sparse array of clothes, I was eager to see the view from the window. The sun was still high in the sky and shone down on a vast lake, two white swans glided across the mirrored water, four cygnets in their wake. I could see a white summer pavilion on the other side of the water, and to one side of the lake was a beautiful garden full of brightly-coloured flowers intermingling with one another.

The whole scene in its entirety was beautifully tranquil and so in contrast to the front of the house. Then on my left out of the corner of my eye I could see that the round tower was adjacent to my room. I was obviously at the top of the house and my window was level with the one that jutted out from the tower, so close to me I could almost touch it.

I shivered involuntarily and went over to the mirror.

Removing my straw bonnet I marvelled at the fact that my thick dark blonde hair had not strayed out of place, the pins which held the back in a twisted knot were still in place.

Replacing my bonnet I decided to take a closer look at the beautiful lake. A walk in the fresh air would do me good after the long journey from London, my unpacking could wait.

As I stepped into the narrow

corridor, Miss Hayward was about to step into the room next to mine, she stopped, one hand on the door knob and a tray balanced precariously on the other. Swiftly I walked over to her and removed the tray from her hand.

'Thank you, Miss Sinclair,' she said quietly.

'Abbey, please call me Abbey,' I urged as I followed Miss Hayward into her room which was a bit larger than mine. She'd made it her own, pictures hung on the walls and a small table by her bed held petite china ornaments. The room looked lived in and was quite pleasant, the bottom of the window was open causing the pink curtains to flutter softly in the warm summer breeze.

'What a delightful room,' I said with honesty.

'Thank you, and please call me Alice.' As she replied, Alice lay the tray on the bed. 'Please join me as you must be hungry after your journey.'

So we sat on the bed sharing Alice's

afternoon tea in almost a companionable silence while looking out over the lake and gardens, the sun shining through the window on us both. Suddenly all fanciful thoughts of gloom and foreboding left me and I felt quite relaxed.

'Why are you here as a companion?' Alice's gentle voice cut into my revelry.

I looked at her for some time before I spoke. 'I needed the post as much for myself as the wage,' I said quietly, my hand toying idly with the teaspoon on the tray.

'And what of your parents?' Alice questioned further.

'Both dead,' I said with a firmness and finality which I felt. 'My mother died of diphtheria when I was nine, I went to live with various aunts and uncles as my father was a seafaring man.'

'Was?' Alice reiterated.

'Yes, he died some three months ago from an illness of the lungs, and I've been looking to secure a suitable position since then,' I replied wistfully.

'You've not thought of marriage then?' Alice asked with interest.

'No, unfortunately not, no man has totally appealed to me, a fair few have had different qualities, but I seek one with them all.' I looked at Alice and laughed. 'You?' she hesitated for a moment before replying.

'There is someone I truly love with all my heart.' Here she stopped and I felt to press her further would be folly for she suddenly seemed back in her own little world.

I thanked her for the tea and as I went to leave turned back to her an intriguing question hovering on my lips.

'Why does Mrs Kershaw wear a veil over her face?' I asked.

'Some accident in the past causes her to hide her scars from the world,' Alice replied vaguely and I realised that to ask her anything else today would be futile.

★　★　★

It took me some time to find my way to the lower floor and locate the servants' entrance, but a kindly young maid in a white mop cap named Maggie showed me the way out. As I stepped outside once more I knew I was at the far side of the house for I could see the tower at the opposite end.

Slowly I walked to the back of the building savouring the warmth of the sun. Reaching the back of the house I marvelled at how different it was from the front. Wisteria flowered on the walls and the glorious scent of roses pervaded my nostrils. A path wound its way to the lake which I proceeded to follow, quite overawed by the beauty of it all.

As I walked along the path I could see the figure of a young man walking ever nearer towards me. He wore no hat on his dark tousled hair and was tall and as I slowed my step I could almost feel the ground move beneath my feet and my heart started to beat faster, why he had this affect on me I could not say, all I knew was I'd never experienced such a feeling before.

'What a pleasant day!' he called out in a strong low masculine voice.

'Why yes, indeed it is,' I managed to utter. As we drew nearer to each other I could see that the stranger had startling blue eyes, very similar to Antony Kershaw's, but while Antony Kershaw's were cold, his were smiling and bright.

'I'm Thomas Craddock,' he said with a slight nod of his head, he smiled displaying his white teeth which were even more prominent because of his tanned skin. 'And you are?' he questioned.

'Abbey Sinclair,' I uttered, all the while being held by the startling blue of his eyes. 'I arrived today to be companion to Mrs Kershaw.'

'Aunt Henry, well I wish you luck, she can be a real tartar,' he admitted his eyes twinkling.

'Why do you call her Henry?' I queried solemnly. 'She told me she hates pet names and insists on calling me Abigail.'

'Does she indeed, I've always called her Henry since I was a child, I'm the errant nephew, by the way.' He laughed as he spoke.

'And do you live here Mr Craddock?' I asked him.

'Only temporarily, I'm here to catalogue the paintings in the long gallery. And please call me Thomas or Tom would be even more to my liking. Shall we take a seat?' As he spoke he indicated a small wooden bench quite near us on the path.

'Why yes,' I agreed like someone in a trance. I warmed to this young man and felt that I had known him for a long time.

'Where do you normally live?' I asked, more for something to say than any real desire to know the answer for I was quite happy that he was at this moment resided at Kerslake Hall.

'I have a small house, Tidwell Cottage near Whitby which is about seven miles from here. Do you know it?'

'The cottage, no,' I replied foolishly, for some reason not knowing what I was saying.

'Whitby, I mean!' he said laughing.

'No, I've lived most of my life in Portsmouth and London, I'm newly arrived here today.' My cheeks flushed as I spoke and I prayed he would not look on me as some dizzy person who didn't know what she was talking about. His next words sent warmth through my whole body.

'Then I shall take you to my humble home and to see the beautiful fishing town of Whitby. Saturday perhaps?' he asked quite seriously. As it was only Monday today I felt as if I could hardly wait.

'Why yes, I'd really like that,' I replied with honesty for I felt strongly that I could trust this man with the laughing blue eyes.

'I shall look forward to our outing, Miss Sinclair, and shall think of it while I'm working.' As he spoke he rose from his seat. 'Apologies, but I must go now. My cousin, Antony, is a hard task master.' So saying he took my hand in his and bending over it left a gentle kiss which sent my pulses racing.

As he made to walk off he looked back at me. 'Don't take Aunt Henry's manner to heart, she's quite a softy really.'

As he walked away I could scarcely believe my good fortune, and sat for a while recalling the whole of the conversation several times. My heart seemed to be singing and when I did get to my feet I practically skipped along the rest of the path around the lake, now and then picking a small pebble up and throwing it in the water as I'd done so many times as a child.

Eventually I reached the far end of the lake and the high wall which surrounded the Hall. On the moor beyond which seemed to stretch endlessly, sheep grazed amongst the heather then I looked back at Kerslake Hall and could see it in it's entirety from end to end. The round tower looked forbidding and as I looked I could pick out the window of my room and that of Alice's too.

My attention was arrested by some movement in the upper window of the tower. I closed my eyes then looked again, but whatever it was had gone. I knew I'd not imagined it for my eyesight was sharp, even at this distance and as I pondered over what it might be in my haste to retrace my steps I fell over something at the edge of the path near to the water, luckily falling on to the ground and not into the water itself.

Picking myself up I looked down at the offending object which was a small wooden plaque, engraved in brass the words, *Phoebe Kershaw Rest in Peace*.

I looked at it for some time trying to work out who Phoebe was and why a plaque in her memory should lie at the edge of the lake. No doubt at some time all would be revealed and the answer to the mystery would become apparent to me. As I walked back to the Hall I put the incident from mind and thought instead of the blue eyes and the smile of Thomas Craddock.

*   *   *

That night tucked up in bed in the darkness I recalled the events of the day, the veil covering my employer's face, the child Emily, my encounter with Tom and the mysterious plaque by the water. I had just drifted off into a peaceful sleep when I was awoken by a piercing, heart wrenching scream seeming to come from behind my bed.

Trembling I got out of bed, looking at the small clock on the table, it was one in the morning. I made my way to the window my legs like jelly. I parted the curtains a little and looked into the window of the tower. Silhouetted by the light of a candle was a woman dressed in white with long hair cascading down her back.

Swiftly I drew the curtains together and climbed back into bed pulling the covers over my head. If it wasn't for

Tom, on the morrow I would be leaving this ghastly place.

After some time I did drift off to sleep but not before I'd asked myself the question, who was the woman in white?

3

When I awoke next morning after a fitful sleep, I realised how terrified I had been in the early hours of the morning. So much so, that I hadn't given much logical thought to the incident. In the light of day, things didn't seem so bad and my sensible head told me that it had been a maid in the tower, but that didn't explain the blood-curdling scream which had awoken me.

I drew back the pale blue curtains and looked at the tower. There was no movement in any of the windows this morning, maybe I'd dreamt it. As I stood there looking, I thought to walk to the tower from the inside and find the entrance to it which surely must be not far from my own door.

Stepping into the corridor, I looked left and right. No-one was in sight although I could hear Emily's voice coming from Alice's room. Walking swiftly to the right and to the end of the corridor, I soon found the sturdy wooden door which must lead to the upper floor of the tower. I needed to climb three stone steps to turn the huge black handle which would raise the latch. I tried to turn it to no avail, the door was shut fast.

'Can I help you, Miss Sinclair?' Mrs Grafton's voice startled me somewhat as I turned guiltily towards her, my one hand still on the latch.

'No, Mrs Grafton. I thought to see where this door leads,' I stammered, negotiating the steps as I spoke.

'The door is no longer used. It leads to the upper floor of the tower, but it is unsafe now.' Did I believe Mrs Grafton's words or my own experience during the night? I thought to believe myself as Mrs Grafton had a sly way with her and I felt that she was annoyed that I had tried to open the door. It remained to be seen what happened during my second night at the Hall.

'I came to ask where you wish to partake of breakfast. I'd be grateful if you'd let someone know the evening before in future,' Mrs Grafton's voice admonished me. I didn't care for her manner and wondered if Mrs Kershaw's abominable attitude had rubbed off on her housekeeper.

'In the kitchen as I did last night and will do in future, if this is acceptable. Thank you.' I found it difficult to remember my manners when dealing with this woman.

'That will be quite acceptable, Miss Sinclair. Now I suggest you run along as it is nearly seven-thirty,' she replied in a bossy manner which I loathed. It was as if she were speaking to Emily and not me, a twenty-five-year-old woman.

'I'll do that, Mrs Grafton,' I said with some sarcasm. 'Could you tell me please when Mrs Kershaw requires me?'

'The mistress sleeps in until twelve o'clock. If you are required this afternoon I will seek you out.' So saying, she turned her back on me and without ceremony entered Miss Hayward's room.

I made my way down to the kitchen feeling much more familiar with the layout of the house. As I approached the door, I could hear the murmur of voices, but as I stepped into the large room, all six at the table were silent, each turning to look at me.

I seated myself at the long wooden table next to Maggie who glanced at me, smiling her sweet smile before continuing with her stodgy porridge.

'Please don't be silent and stop talking on my account,' I addressed them all.

'Would you like some porridge, Miss?' asked Cook who was a rounded homely looking woman. I'd learned the previous evening her name was Ada. I glanced down at Maggie's dish.

'No thank you, toast would be very nice, please,' I said politely.

'And a nice strong, hot cup of tea, I'll

be bound.' As she spoke, Ada busied herself at the large black kitchen range, pouring tea into a large white mug from the largest black china teapot I'd ever seen.

'What were you talking about before I came in?' I looked from one to the other. 'I can keep secrets, I assure you.'

'It's no secret,' said Maggie.

'Maggie, I'll thank you not to speak unless spoken to,' said Cook sharply, looking at me with keen eyes obviously weighing up the situation.

'You have an honest face, Miss,' she said at length, handing me the mug and a plate of toast. 'So I'll tell you for you'll surely hear it anyway. They dragged another young woman out of the lake this morning. Young Gladys White from the village, pretty bairn she were, only sixteen years old.' Ada sighed and I looked at her with some astonishment.

'When you say another, I take it you mean she's not the first,' I questioned, my breakfast quite forgotten.

'Aye, she's the second in the past six months, apart from . . . ' Here she stopped and took a deep breath.

'Apart from who?' As I asked the question, I felt I knew the answer.

'Young mistress, but it's not for me to say.' Ada shrugged her shoulders and walked back to the range, conversation over.

As I left the kitchen, I mulled all this over in my mind. Two young women from the village, plus I assumed Antony Kershaw's wife. Were they all accidents or of malicious intent? To think I'd walked around the lake yesterday and marvelled at its beauty. I shuddered at the thought; and perhaps this would explain Harry's reticence to bring me to the Hall on my arrival, quite a mystery.

As it happened, it wasn't Mrs Grafton who sought me out, but Antony Kershaw. He stopped me as I made my way back to my room, intent on seeing what was happening at the lake.

'Miss Sinclair.' His voice startled me.

'I wonder, could you help out at the schoolroom in the village for a couple of days?'

'Yes, of course,' I stammered, bemused at his request. 'But what of your mother?' I asked with some alarm, thinking of the indomitable Mrs Kershaw.

'Do not worry. I shall instruct the housekeeper to tell the mistress where we are. I just need to show you the schoolroom today. It is tomorrow you are needed as schoolmistress. Miss Anderson has to visit her sick mother for a couple of days.'

I watched him as he spoke, his blue eyes were startling but cold. His clothes today were brown not grey so that was another fanciful thought on my arrival that everyone wore grey and I wondered what the lovely Alice Hayward wore today.

As if in answer to my question, Alice appeared dressed in blue which caused me to feel very dowdy in comparison. Emily ran to her father who embraced her and then put her from him as she eagerly asked if he would walk with her.

'Not today, Emily. I have to take Miss Sinclair to the village,' he said firmly.

'Can I come, please?' pleaded Emily.

'You have your lessons. Maybe we can walk this afternoon. Now go with your governess.' At his words, Emily looked downcast, but she took the hand of Miss Hayward who had been watching the scene in respectful silence.

As they walked away, Antony Kershaw addressed me once more. 'I'll meet you in the hall in half-an-hour, Miss Sinclair, and we'll make our way to Beckmoor.' With which words he was gone.

★   ★   ★

Hastily I made my way to my room to change my dress, for I felt really drab, but before I removed my grey attire, I looked out of the window. There was one policeman by the lake, guarding a bundle covered with a blanket. Quickly I turned away, wondering who had found the poor unfortunate Gladys. I was to learn later that it had been Thomas.

Dressed in a pale green day dress with my straw boater in place, I made my way to the hall. How different it looked this morning I thought. Sun streamed through the glass panel above the door and the two windows each side of it. I could now see all the highly polished furniture set against the walls, including a beautiful tall hat rack by the door. I looked quickly into the mirror set in the middle of it.

'I'm sure you'll do, Miss Sinclair.' Antony Kershaw's voice came to me from some little distance away and my cheeks flushed.

'I do hope so,' I countered with some embarrassment. For some reason I felt uncomfortable today in this man's presence and was not looking forward to the journey with him.

A pony and trap had been brought to the front and once more I stepped on to the gravel path. Mr Kershaw helped me

39

into the trap beside him. I needn't have worried. He was silent all the way while I looked around at the scenery which was unchanging until we reached the small village. A row of white thatched cottages cut their way defiantly through the surrounding moor.

I observed a blacksmith's and a communal tap where a couple of women were filling large buckets. As we approached, they turned away, for what reason I could not understand. But very soon I was to find out. I was somewhat surprised when the trap pulled up beside the village church.

'But I thought we were to go to the schoolroom,' I uttered.

'Come, you will see.' As he spoke, Mr Kershaw helped me alight. We walked through the lychgate and along the path flanked either side by many grey moss covered tombstones.

In one corner I could see a large mausoleum which I was keen to look at closely. I followed Mr Kershaw through the church door and stepped on to the slab floor. It felt cold in here and smelled damp despite the warmth of the early morning sun and I wondered why he had brought me here.

On the right hand side of the church entrance was a low wooden door. My companion lifted the latch and I followed him up the stone steps which led us into a small room.

Here the sun did shine through a window and five small children sat cross-legged on the wooden floor, slates and chalks in their little hands and the girls wearing white starched aprons over their dresses.

In the corner, writing on a blackboard, was a schoolmistress dressed in black, the braids of her fair hair entwined into a knot at the back of her head with a white lace cap covering her head. I gasped in surprise.

'I've never seen a room like this before above a church porch. I'm sure it's unique,' I enthused.

'It may well be, Miss Sinclair. Let me introduce you to Miss Anderson.' The schoolteacher stopped writing on the blackboard and inclined her head towards me.

'Pleased to make your acquaintance, Miss Sinclair, and please meet my five young charges, Rosie, Clara, Victoria, Michael and Danny.' She indicated the children one by one and as each name was spoken they all replied, 'Hello, Miss Sinclair.' I was quite touched by the whole scene.

'Good morning, children,' I replied with enthusiasm. I knew I was going to enjoy this new experience. There was a list of lessons for each day, mainly spelling, writing and arithmetic and each day they were to be taken on a short walk across the moor.

Mr Kershaw and I left the schoolroom with the children's farewells ringing in our ears. It was nice to step into the sunshine. I looked up into the sky which was a perfect blue. Another beautiful day was in store and I wondered how bleak the moor would look on a grey and rainy day.

'I have to visit the general store for some comfits for Emily,' Antony Kershaw's voice drifted across to me.

'Very well. May I look around the churchyard while you are gone, please? I like to look at names engraved on headstones for they all tell a story.'

This was true. What I didn't want to tell him was that I intended to take a closer look at the mausoleum for I was sure it was the Kershaws' monument.

'That will be fine, Miss Sinclair. I'll be about three-quarters of an hour. Don't trip over anything,' he said solicitously and then added, 'The last thing I need is a female with a sprained ankle.'

I watched his retreating figure and didn't know what to make of him. On the one hand he was pleasant and friendly, on the other he was aloof and distant. I walked in and out of the gravestones, weaving my way slowly towards the monument in the corner.

I came upon a fairly new grave with just a wooden cross at its head. Bending

43

over so I could see the name carved in the wood, I read, *Annie Blake. Aged 16*.

A woman tending a grave nearby watched me as I stood up once more. Her arms were folded as she watched my progress towards her intently. 'Morning,' I called to her, 'Another lovely day.'

'For some, maybe,' she replied abruptly, 'But certainly not for Gladys White's family.' The girl who'd been pulled from the lake at Kerslake Hall, I thought.

'I'm really sorry,' I said sincerely, for while I didn't know the girl, I felt compassion for her family.

'Are you working up at the Hall then?' she questioned.

'Yes indeed, but I arrived only yesterday.' As I spoke, I had neared the woman and stopped before her.

'You don't really know the Master then? Though I saw you with him just now. Thought you were one of his women until I saw you closer and realised you weren't wearing an expensive gown.' I was shocked at this revelation.

'You are right, I'm not one of his women,' I said, indignation rising in me.

'Just as well, for he has a cruel steak in him, that one. He killed his lovely young wife as sure as I'm standing here talking to you, and I wouldn't doubt that he killed poor Annie and Gladys, too, in his lake. God rest their souls.'

To say I was astonished was an understatement. I was for once tongue-tied.

'Oh, yes,' she continued, 'You watch that one.'

'Thank you for telling me,' was all I managed to say and then I watched her walk to the lychgate, swinging the watering can she carried to and fro.

As I walked towards the corner of the churchyard, my mind was in a whirl, names of people were racing through my brain, Antony, Thomas, Miss Anderson, Alice and Emily.

Poor Emily, who loved her father so much and was so innocent. I could hardly believe it and wouldn't believe it. He was innocent until proved guilty and there again, was he innocent?

I'd reached my goal. The mausoleum was indeed the Kershaws' final resting place. It was tall and stately, rising out of the ground into a triangular peak which was intricately carved. I read many names and dates, some going back to the seventeenth century, all Kershaws except one.

The name jumped out at me, Albert Miles. Died January the 10th aged 30 years. The inscription puzzled me. Why would a Miles be buried in a Kershaw grave? Then I spotted what I think I'd been looking for.

Phoebe Kershaw. Beloved wife of Antony Kershaw. Mother of Emily. Died July 15th, 1888. Aged 28 years.

The day I'd arrived at Kerslake Hall, July the fifteenth, and Gladys had died that day. I was anxious to know what date Annie died, but I wasn't to find out today, for Antony Kershaw's voice arrested my attention.

'So you found the Kershaw mausoleum then.' As he spoke, I turned round to look at him and took a step back. Was I looking at a loving son, husband and father? Or a murderer?

4

Mrs Grafton pounced on me as soon as I stepped into the hall on my return. 'The Mistress wishes to see you now,' she said with a look of triumph on her face.

'I'll follow you then, Mrs Grafton.' Once more the housekeeper led me to Mrs Kershaw's sitting-room, the corridor didn't seem so dark today.

'Abigail Sinclair,' Henrietta's voice boomed out, 'It's not enough that I have to rise early to be questioned by a young policeman, bombastic man. But that's by the by, more importantly I find that my most recent employee, namely you, is riding around the countryside with my son who tells me that you are to teach in the schoolroom for two days.' As she spoke the old lady pointed her cane at me.

'But,' I interrupted.

'And why are you wearing a green dress when I specifically requested that you wear grey, tell me that?'

'I,' but I was not to be given the chance to explain.

'Well Abigail, take the week off why don't you, and please don't interrupt me again. You are dismissed from my presence for the time being at least.'

As I left the room I felt inclined to slam the door shut, but thought better of it, for bad manners would get me nowhere. I'd been well and truly trounced by an old lady who had left me bristling with anger.

I was not therefore in a good frame of mind when I bumped headlong into Thomas Craddock.

'Begging your pardon Miss Sinclair,' he apologised, and then took my shoulders holding me at arms length. 'Why, you look positively in the doldrums. Now what can I do to rectify that?' His words brought a smile to my face, also the touch of his hands on my shoulders was very pleasant. 'That's better,' he sighed, cupping his hand under my chin and turning my face to look at him. 'What ails you?'

'Your aunt,' I replied peevishly.

'Dear Aunt Henry? She blows cold air trust me and don't take it to heart,' he soothed.

'Why no, I shouldn't let her spoil the day,' I said in agreement.

'I'm afraid Miss Sinclair, the day is already spoiled by what I discovered in the lake this morning.' At these words he looked very serious.

'Yes, I did hear at breakfast time, but did not know until now who had found poor Gladys,' I said, touching his arm in a gesture of sympathy.

'It was rather a gruesome find, the poor girl was lying across the edge of the lake with her head bobbing on the water.'

At these words I felt physically sick and could imagine the whole scene. 'You look rather pale Miss Sinclair, I fear I've distressed you. Now let us put it out of our minds, how about coming with me for a walk to Thursdon Abbey?' he suggested with enthusiasm.

'Yes, I'd like that, and as I've been given the week off I'm sure no harm is done,' I laughed.

'Now, that's better. Sit on this chair while I persuade Ada to pack up some sandwiches and lemonade.' I did as he bid thinking he could charm the birds out of the trees.

★   ★   ★

Despite being instructed to use the servants' entrance, I found myself stepping out of the main door for the second time that day, with Thomas by my side and the sun beating down. It was hard to believe that a young girl had died so recently in the vicinity.

'Do you think she was murdered?' I asked Thomas, for I was keen to know his opinion.

'It's hard to tell,' he answered, 'for one thing, who would want to kill her and what was she doing in the grounds of Kerslake Hall? I found her near the plaque Antony had placed in Phoebe's memory. For that is where Phoebe was found, not far from the summer pavilion. She could have tripped over the plaque if it was dark.' As Thomas talked we found ourselves outside the boundary of the Hall and following a hilly dirt track.

'And what of Annie?' I asked.

'I do believe she was found in the same place in similar circumstances, most odd, but don't worry your pretty head about it today.' As he spoke we reached the top of the incline and I could see before me the ruined abbey.

'What a beautiful scene,' I said out loud, the words escaping my lips for indeed it was quite picturesque with the ruined walls and only the blue sky for a roof surrounded by green grass and the moor.

As we continued walking, Thomas carrying the small wicker picnic basket in one hand and steadying me at the elbow with his free hand, little did he know that this was a scene that I had dreamed of for so long. To walk with a handsome gentleman on a summer's day.

I fervently hoped nothing would spoil it, not now or ever. We ran in and out of the ruins like children, the soft grass beneath our feet. We sat together on the grass eating sandwiches and sipping lemonade. I was hot and removed my straw hat longing to unpin my hair and let it loose.

'You have such beautiful hair,' Thomas said softly as if he'd guessed what I was thinking. He looked at his silver pocket watch and I knew that this lovely interlude would soon be over. 'It's two o'clock, we must go.' So saying he rose to his feet and caught my hand to help me up.

'It's been so nice,' I said politely.

'It has indeed and I look forward to our outing on Saturday.'

The picnic packed away we walked slowly back to the Hall. Thomas went through the main door bidding me farewell and I made my way to the rear of the building as I intended to sit in the rose garden for a while. I felt quite lost without Thomas at my side.

★ ★ ★

As I reached the spot which led to the lake I looked sadly at the water, but all seemed normal now with the swans gliding across it and no-one else in sight. I looked at the summer pavilion and hoped that one day soon I would sit in there. It was fortunate I didn't know then how soon it would be nor in what circumstances.

Stepping into the rose garden I realised I wasn't alone, for Miss Hayward and Emily were sitting on one of the many wooden benches. Miss Hayward held a pretty sunshade over her.

At the sight of me she raised her hand, I walked towards them surrounded by a beautiful riot of colour, red, pink, yellow and peach-coloured roses the fragrance overwhelming.

'It is all right for me to sit with you for a while?' I asked Alice.

'Of course,' and as she spoke she gently patted the seat, 'please play with your hoop Emily, but keep to the path.' The child did as she was bid bowling a wooden hoop along with each step, her shiny dark ringlets dancing up and down.

'Have you heard the awful news, Abbey?'

'About Gladys you mean? Yes, at breakfast,' I replied, quite pleased that Alice had used my Christian name. 'It's quite a mystery I believe, were you here when Annie was found?'

'Yes, I've been here since the young Mrs Kershaw had her tragic accident,' Alice said quietly.

'But she too was found in the lake, or so I understand,' I said looking at Alice for confirmation.

'That is true. What worries me is who will be next. If I wasn't so fond of the child I would think of leaving this place.'

At Alice's words I mulled over whether I could confide in her about the events of last night but decided instead to try a different course.

'The last two companions to the older Mrs Kershaw, why did they leave so soon?' I asked.

'I don't really know, they were both older in years than yourself. Mrs Kershaw doesn't care for younger women or so I've come to believe. All I know is that neither of them was here for many days. Thinking about it, the one lady mentioned a light in the tower to Mrs Grafton, I can say no more as Emily is coming back,' she said quickly.

'Hello Emily,' I greeted the child.

'Miss Sinclair, it's my birthday next week and I always have a party and as I'm to be ten, Papa says I can have it in the evening, will you come?' she asked enthusiastically.

'I doubt it, Emily, for one thing I haven't got an invitation,' I replied.

'Well, I invite you, Miss Sinclair. So please come.' I had no time to reply as

Emily ran off bowling her hoop again.

'Yes you must come, Abbey.' Alice's voice broke into my thoughts. 'It's only us grown-ups with Emily and she likes us to dress up.'

'How delightful, what day does it fall on?' I asked with some interest, for no doubt Thomas would be there.

'Next Thursday. It will be more fun with you there, I feel quite lost sometimes among the family, I only wish Emily had some friends, but it appears no-one from the village will come to the Hall,' Alice said and I could see she was slipping back into her daydreaming again. 'I must get back for the child's afternoon tea. Emily,' she called and the child ran obediently to her.

After they'd gone I thought about what Alice had said during her conversation. The party was of interest, but uppermost in my mind were the words, 'What worries me is who will be next.' I had to admit that the thought had not crossed my mind before, but I vowed now to be vigilant at all times.

It was getting hot, but unlike Alice I was without a sunshade and I felt lost as to what to do. If I could seek out Antony Kershaw, maybe he would be kind enough to allow me to make use of the library if indeed there was a library at Kerslake Hall.

I decided to throw caution to the wind and enter by the side door, praying as I did so that the daunting figure of Mrs Grafton would not be around. As I stepped into the hall once more I needn't have feared and I was in luck, for Mr Kershaw was crossing the hall, his step resounding on the black and white tiles.

'Mr Kershaw,' I approached him, 'please don't think me forward, but please could I make use of your library and find something to read?'

'But of course, Miss Sinclair. The library here is hardly used except by myself which is quite a sad state of affairs. Please feel free to sit there whenever you wish.' He spoke the words quite kindly and I really could not make out what kind of person he was.

'Thank you so much, there is just one thing, I don't know where to locate it.' At this he laughed, the laughter not quite reaching his eyes.

'Mrs Grafton,' my heart sank for the housekeeper had just stepped into the hall, I could hear the keys jangling at her waist, 'please be kind enough to show Miss Sinclair to the library. I have given my permission for her to use the room whenever she desires,' he instructed.

'Yes, Sir,' Mrs Grafton said pleasantly enough, and so once more I followed the silent figure in grey along another corridor. She did not speak or open the door, but indicated the room with her hand and gave me such a venomous look before she retraced her steps that I felt as though she had slapped me in the face.

* * *

The library was cool and out of the sun for which I was thankful. It was a large room with books lining the walls from top to bottom. Under the long window was a small square table with a large book placed on top of it, I was intrigued by the size of the book more than anything hence I went over to take a closer look.

It was a family bible, with the most unusual cover I had ever seen. It had been embroidered in bright colours of red, green, yellow and blue, whoever had stitched it had worked on it beautifully. I deliberated as to whether to open it or not as I thought it may hold details of the Kershaw family. I was more than curious to know how old Thomas Craddock was.

While deciding what to do, I searched the shelves for a suitable book to entertain me. A cream-coloured volume of *Vanity Fair* caught my eye and I picked it out then sat on a chair to look at it. I made a quick decision to borrow the book and look through the bible before anyone came in.

Turning the lovely cover I could see there was indeed a list of family births, marriages and deaths from 1750. I quickly turned the page to find the more recent entries, at the bottom of the list was Emily, born July 25th 1880 to Antony and Phoebe Kershaw.

Above I could see Thomas, born 1865 to Mary and Thomas Craddock. So he was the same age as me, I mused, and was about to close the bible when Henrietta Kershaw's name caught my eye.

She had been born in 1825 and had been born a Kershaw. This revelation surprised me somewhat and I quickly went down again to Antony, he had been born in 1855 to Henrietta Kershaw and the sadly departed Albert Miles. Quickly I closed the bible admiring once more the cover, I felt as though I'd been intrusive and regretted prying into the family affairs.

Leaving the library, the copy of

Vanity Fair in my hand, I thought that Henrietta Kershaw had no cause for all her airs and graces and sharp words, for if the bible were to be believed and it couldn't be wrong she was indeed a Miss. For all my prying I had indeed uncovered a trump card.

Later that evening in my room, I left the lamp burning deciding to read and be awake should there be any movement again in the tower. I read for three hours, my head eventually nodding, my eyes weary for sleep. When I was brought to by a movement behind my bed, someone was climbing the stairs.

I slammed the novel shut and laid it on the table. Looking at the clock I could see it was five to one. I braced myself for the scream and when it came I put my fingers in my ears hardly able to bear the shrillness of it. Quickly I slipped on my robe and as quietly as I could opened my bedroom door, then stepped into the corridor making my way to the door of the tower.

As I climbed the three stone steps I

could see that the heavy door was slightly ajar. This fact alone caused me to tremble and with shaking hands I opened the door farther to enable me to take a look behind it. Thankfully the door slid open quietly and I could see stone steps to the upper floor.

The staircase curved at one point and I bravely decided to ascend the steps, the glow of candlelight from above lighting my way. Half of me wanted to retreat and the other half of me, although I was afraid of what I might encounter, pressed on.

I reached the bend in the staircase and stood suddenly still hardly daring to breathe, so much so that I clapped a hand to my mouth for I could see the room above only three steps away and I could see the woman in a long white night-gown, light-coloured wavy hair cascading down her back to her waist.

She was slight of build and appeared to be praying as I could hear the murmur of her voice and caught the word, *Lord*, twice. I couldn't stay for who was she and what would she do if she found me there? If she had a mind to she could push me down the stairs. With this thought, as hastily as I could without her hearing, I descended the steps and gently pushed the door to allow me access to the corridor once more.

I practically fled to my room, closing the door quietly behind me and looking through the curtains, could see no light in the tower.

I'd obviously left just in time but I knew without a doubt that this time I'd not imagined it or dreamed it and as I snuggled under the cotton sheet I prayed that next time I would possess more courage to solve the mystery.

5

I enjoyed my first day at the school, the children were delightful, very obedient and friendly, all except Clara who was quiet all day and didn't join in verbally with any of the lessons. At the end of the day I took her to one side.

'Is something bothering you, Clara, for you've not spoken to me all day,' I questioned. Her answer was to shrug her shoulders and look away. 'How old are you?' I asked gently.

'Eight, Miss,' she replied reluctantly.

'Perhaps you don't like me and are missing Miss Anderson,' I said.

'I do like you Miss, but Ma and Pa told me I wasn't to have anything to do with you as you live at the Hall,' she said quietly not looking me in the face. So, I thought, even the children couldn't escape the animosity towards the Kershaw family. Quickly I cleaned the blackboard and tidied up, then placing my bonnet on I took hold of Clara's hand.

'I'm walking you home Clara as I wish to speak to your mother and father,' I said firmly. The child didn't object and led me to one of the white cottages in the village. A woman was on her knees polishing the brass step at the front door.

She turned her head around at our arrival and I was quite shocked, although relatively young she had dark circles under her troubled eyes and her face was as white as the sheets on my bed. Getting up she pulled Clara from me placing a protective arm round the girl's shoulder.

'What do you want?' she asked with hatred in her voice, 'go home where you belong.'

'Strictly speaking,' I said quietly, 'Kerslake Hall isn't my home and I am not a Kershaw, and have indeed been here only two days.'

'That's as may be, but you were there

when my Gladys was found.' Her voice broke as she spoke the words and my heart missed a beat for I had not expected Clara to be Gladys' sister.

'Mrs White, I am so sorry.' So saying I went to her and put my arm gently around her shoulder. I half expected her to push me away, but instead she cried, blowing her nose on the hem of her apron. As she calmed down she looked at me, 'Have you any bairns?' she asked.

'No,' I said simply.

'Well when you have you'll understand. A good girl Gladys were, I still can't believe she's gone,' she said sniffing into her apron once more.

'Mrs White, I understand how you must be feeling,' I said, an idea forming in my mind, 'would you allow Clara to come up to the Hall next Thursday for Emily's party?' At my words Mrs White looked at me aghast.

'What! And have her murdered too!'

'Not at all, I want you to see all is not bad at Kerslake Hall, and young Emily has no friends,' I spoke with encourage-ment.

'I'll think on it,' she conceded, 'and I'll have to ask my husband, I doubt he'll be agreeable.'

'Yes, please think about it and I'll call on you next week if I may.' My voice was soothing as I spoke and as she stepped through the door with Clara she looked back at me.

'You do that, Miss,' she said grudg-ingly.

* * *

Later, back in my bedroom while freshening up my face with some cold water, I thought how foolish I had been to invite Clara to the Hall and that I would have to speak to Antony Kershaw about it as it wasn't my place to hand out invitations to anyone.

But my thoughts had been with both Emily and Clara, having a strong feeling that they would get on well together.

There was a tap on the door before I had a chance to change my grey dress for the pale green one. Without any ado or by your leave Mrs Grafton appeared in the doorway.

'The Mistress wishes to see you now,' she instructed, a sly smile to her lips as she spoke.

'If that is so, then I had better come with you now,' I said, pleased that I hadn't yet changed after all.

As I entered Mrs Kershaw's sitting-room I was more than surprised to see Thomas standing there, his hands behind his back, he was just as surprised to see me.

'Miss Sinclair!' he exclaimed smiling at me and then looking at his aunt who sat upright in her armchair, the cat, Charles, on her lap.

'So Aunt Henry, why have you summoned the both of us?' he asked with his devil may care manner.

'I have brought the two of you here as it had been brought to my attention that the pair of you have been seen walking together to the Abbey and indeed sharing a picnic on the grass. What have you to say for yourselves?' Henrietta Kershaw's harsh voice boomed out.

'There is no harm done, Aunt Henry,' replied Thomas, somewhat irritated I could tell.

'I will not have you associating with my paid help. For one thing it is unseemly and secondly it displeases me,' his aunt shouted back at him.

'And just what does please you, Aunt Henry?' I felt Thomas had gone too far at these words.

'I'll thank you not to speak to me like that and don't call me by that name, you know it irks me,' Mrs Kershaw retaliated.

'Well I have every intention of taking Abbey to Tidwell on Saturday, whether you like it or not!' Thomas's voice was rising and he tapped his foot slowly on the floor as he spoke.

'But she's as poor as a church mouse!' At these words I interrupted her.

'And how do you know this, pray?' I'd found my tongue in the old lady's presence at last. 'I'll have you know I'm not completely destitute, for I have a wealthy aunt.'

'Enough!' the old lady shouted, banging her fist on the table and shoving the sleeping cat off her lap. 'I forbid you to see each other outside the confines of this house and if you do I shall dismiss you, Miss Sinclair.'

At this she pointed a bony finger towards me. I looked at Mrs Kershaw and Thomas then, picking up my skirts, I fled from the room, tears threatening to fall. Thomas was intent on following me, but I heard the old lady shout, 'Stay!'

I would seek him out later. It was because of him I stayed and I admitted to myself that I could not bear not to see him and spend time with him as we had on the day we walked to the abbey. As I ran I bumped straight into Mrs Grafton, almost knocking her over.

She took one look at my tear-stained

face and smiled. I realised then that it was her who had told Mrs Kershaw of my outing with Thomas. I ran straight past her and out of the main door.

Mrs Grafton's voice ringing in my ears, 'Miss Sinclair, use the servants' entrance.' But I didn't give a fig for servants' entrances, Mrs Henrietta Kershaw or Kerslake Hall, all I cared about was Thomas; and then I thought of Emily who had invited me to her party. I stopped running and found myself on the dirt track leading to the abbey.

* * *

It was late afternoon, the sky was blue and the sun shining, a sun which didn't reach my heart. I stopped at the top of the track and looked down at the ruined abbey. The scene before me hadn't changed, but in the last hour all my hopes had been dashed by a bitter old lady who obviously loathed seeing people happy; but was it really so bad I asked myself.

What was the worst that could happen? I could be dismissed, if I were that would mean I could be with Thomas, but where would I go and how would I support myself?

I was amazed at my thoughts, was I really in love? And I felt sure I was, our meeting had been love at first sight. I could tell myself this, but alas not the recipient of my affections, but I felt better at the thought.

Walking slowly back to the house I decided to seek out Thomas who would no doubt be in the long gallery working at this time of day. On entering the house once more I realised that I had no idea where the long gallery was, but guessed it to be on the floor above.

Stepping into the hall I looked around me and as no-one was about, quickly climbed the wide staircase. On reaching the first landing I decided which way to turn and took the left-hand corridor as this was the longest side of the house as the front door was not central to the building.

Opening the door I knew I'd made the right choice for I stepped into a very long room with paintings covering the walls. As my eyes adjusted to the light I could see Thomas halfway down the room. I ran to him, my feet noisy on the polished floorboards beneath, as I neared his silent figure he caught me to him and in that moment I knew he felt the same.

'Oh Thomas!' I said breathlessly, 'she can't keep us apart can she?' I looked at him for some reassurance.

'I won't let her, I promise,' he said freeing the pins at the back of my head, my hair falling over my shoulders. I found myself in a compromising position.

'What if someone comes in?' I said with some sense of alarm.

'No-one will come here except perhaps Antony.' As Thomas spoke he ran his hand over my blonde hair.

'Antony!' I exclaimed, twisting my

hair back into a knot and replacing the pins to hold it in place as best I could.

Thomas laughed, 'I mean you no harm or dishonour,' he said.

'Is it right that two people from different walks in life be drawn to each other. Me poor, you wealthy?' I asked him seriously.

'But you have a rich aunt,' he teased.

'Indeed I do, my father's last remaining sister who had no children, she wanted me to go and live with her, but I was intent on finding my own way through life.' My voice was wistful as I spoke.

'I'm glad you have,' said Thomas seriously, 'for I've never before met anyone like you.' His voice was for once serious although his lovely eyes sparkled with mischief.

'May I look at the pictures?' I asked him. 'For I am very fond of art.'

'But of course, I'll guide you round,' he said with some enthusiasm. I was to learn he was very knowledgeable in his field.

'It is a very long room,' I observed, for indeed it was.

'Yes, it stretches the whole length of the house from the main door to the tower, and see this here?' He stopped at a bare piece of the stone wall, bending a little he looked through what appeared to be a slit in the stone. 'Look through here and tell me what you can see,' he urged me.

There was no need for me to bend as Thomas had done, and looking through the tiny gap in the wall I gasped in surprise.

'Goodness, I can see one side of the hall and the main door.'

For indeed I could, and even as I looked I saw Alice walk across the black and white tiles and then disappear out of the door causing a slant of light to fall on the polished floor. I idly wondered where she was going without Emily. I looked at Thomas. 'What a novel idea,' I enthused.

'Hardly novel, Abbey. It's a squint and has been there for over three hundred years,' he explained.

'Is the house that old then?' I said somewhat surprised. 'It doesn't look that old.'

'But it is. I'm very interested in antiquities, houses, churches, books and paintings,' he said. This was obviously the one thing that he was passionate about and I was pleased that I was getting to know about him.

★ ★ ★

We walked together down the row of paintings, some large, some small and also some likeness, of people I'd never know, miniatures painted with care for a loved one. There was a picture of Kerslake Hall, painted in 1750. Looking at it brought to mind my arrival, was it really only three days ago?

I knew now why the house had seemed so familiar then, for Mr Lang had a copy of the painting hung in his office.

I stopped in front of a very

commanding portrait of a young dark-haired woman, ringlets fell each side of her face, her complexion perfect with rosy cheeks. She wore a cream silk gown adorned with small violet flowers and a prettily-painted fan in one hand.

'Who is this?' I asked Thomas, too entranced to look at the brass plaque beneath.

'It is Aunt Henry in her younger days,' he replied, and I was quite taken aback for this young woman was beautiful and I felt a sudden sympathy for the older Henrietta Kershaw.

'Now you have told me I can see that Emily has some of her features, especially the dark hair and the small pert mouth.' I could hardly believe that this was the same woman that had berated us earlier.

'Well it is, I can assure you.' And he showed me the plaque to prove it, which read, *Henrietta Kershaw 1854*. 'Now let us talk of ourselves.' He insisted taking my arm and leading me towards the door.

'It's nearly six o'clock,' I exclaimed looking at my fob watch. 'The time has just flown by today and I have to be in the kitchen in the next five minutes.'

'Just time for me to say that we will still go to visit Whitby on Saturday if you are willing.' As he asked the question he gently touched my cheek with the back of his hand.

'Indeed I am, for if I am to be banished from the house I know it will be worth it,' I teased laughing up at him.

'Well then, I shall meet you in the pony and trap outside the gates at 9 a.m.' So saying he took my hand gently kissing the palm which sent a shiver through my whole being.

'I shall be there I promise.' Praying silently that no-one would stop us.

⋆ ⋆ ⋆

Later, making my way to my room after supper, my thought was to find a suitable dress in my wardrobe for Emily's party. After my interlude with Thomas in the long gallery I felt so much happier and had a spring in my step again.

The sun had moved across the sky leaving just a ray of light on the wardrobe which appeared to light my way. Opening the door I looked at my sparse array of dresses hung on the rail, deciding on which one would be suitable and alluring.

I picked out my best dress of pale blue, it was made of a light cotton material with a rounded neck-line, puffed sleeves to the elbow and a slightly flared skirt. Quickly I removed my shabby grey dress and put on the blue one.

The cotton felt cool against my skin and as I looked in the mirror at my reflection I realised that if I could find a haberdashery shop in Whitby I could purchase some silk flowers for the shoulder and waistline of the dress to follow the fashion of the day.

Also a matching flower in my hair could look quite fetching, with this thought in mind I felt so much better and looked forward to Emily's party. I was about to remove the dress when there was a tap at the door.

It couldn't be Mrs Grafton for she would have stepped in without invitation, how I loathed that woman. Opening the door I could see it was Alice and drew to one side so she could enter.

'What a delightful dress,' Alice observed, 'and the colour suits you,' she complimented me.

'Thank you, I intend to wear it to Emily's birthday party,' I explained and told her my intention to stitch the silk flowers on to enhance the dress once I'd been able to purchase some.

'A cream colour would look quite fetching,' said the governess walking across to sit on my bed.

'It's pleasant to have you call on me,' I said. 'Was there a purpose for your visit?'

'I wish to know your thoughts about Gladys.' At her words I thought of Clara.

'To be honest I have no idea, except that a woman in the village suggested it was Antony Kershaw.' I said innocently.

'Antony, but that is rubbish!' As Alice spoke she stood up pacing the floor quite distraught. I hadn't expected my words to cause such a reaction.

'I'm sorry if I've upset you, that is the last thing I wanted to do,' I uttered, hoping my words would calm her and realising that Alice was a volatile person.

'Antony Kershaw is a good man, he's been very kind to me and he adores Emily,' she defended him.

'And what of his wife? Did she die in suspicious circumstances?' I asked.

'Certainly not. It was a tragic accident. Apparently Pheobe walked around the lake each evening before she retired for the night. This particular day there had been a lot of rain and she slipped on the mud and fell into the water. It is a very deep lake and Pheobe could not swim. By the time the alarm was raised it was too late.' Alice recounted the tale with some emphasis on the word accident.

'Who told you this?' I asked tentatively.

'Mr Kershaw himself on the day I arrived to take up my position as governess to Emily. He wished to put the record straight for he knows there are many in the village who point an accusing finger at him. This angers me.'

She indeed looked angry I thought and had the feeling that this was a true account of Pheobe's demise. But it didn't explain the deaths of Annie and Gladys. I'd not given it a lot of thought, but thinking about it now someone must have lured them to Kerslake Hall with some false promise.

There were only two men at the Hall now, Mr Kershaw and Thomas. Lord forbid it was him! Then came the thought that Thomas had not been here when Annie died, so unless it was a member of staff like the gardener or handyman the finger did point to Antony Kershaw.

He always did seem like a man with something on his mind, time would tell and I prayed it would be soon, for no female was safe until the culprit was apprehended.

Placing my blue dress back in the wardrobe after Alice had left, and ensuring the skirt of it was straight so it didn't crease, I spied an envelope in the bottom of the wardrobe. Swiftly I bent to pick it up and sitting on the bed I looked at it.

There was no name on the front cover so I opened and read the words on the sheet of paper inside, and this is what it read:

Whoever sleeps in this room and reads this, I want you to know that I too, have heard the steps on the stairs and the scuffling behind the bed. The worse thing is the piercing scream that comes some nights. I am so fearful as to who it is that I can no longer stay, but wish you well. This is a strange household and I shall be glad to leave it. Maybe you should go also before some harm befalls you.

Martha.

As I looked down at the words, I realised Martha had been more frightened than I and was she right? Should I leave now? But then there was Thomas.

I tucked the letter in a drawer of the dressing table and tried to forget it. I was so tired after my eventful day, in fact each of my days had been eventful, but I fell into a restful sleep before one o'clock, but was awoken, not by a scream, but by a scuffling sound in the tower, almost as though someone was moving furniture. I listened for some time but the sound ceased and all was quiet.

I drifted again into a peaceful slumber, thinking of Martha's note, and then dreaming of Thomas and his lips on mine. How I wished that soon it would be reality.

6

Saturday dawned and I could see by the sky that it was going to be a glorious day. I decided to wear the mauve skirt and jacket I'd worn on the day of my arrival as I felt no other dress would be suitable for the occasion.

With breakfast over, I took Maggie to one side. 'Should anyone ask for me,' I confided, 'I am spending the day at Whitby. No-one else knows.'

'Well I hope you have a nice time,' said Maggie, eyes like saucers, 'are you going alone, Miss?' she asked as an afterthought.

'No, I am spending the day with Thomas Craddock, only please tell no-one,' I implored her.

'I promise, Miss,' pledged Maggie, and I knew I could trust her.

As I left the kitchen I had the misfortune to encounter Mrs Grafton, who completely spoilt the moment.

'Ah, Miss Sinclair, the Mistress wishes you to read to her this afternoon in her sitting-room at two o'clock,' she informed me.

'I'll be there.' I said, knowing full-well I would not be back, but I was willing to suffer Henrietta Kershaw's wrath for a day with her nephew, and although I wasn't used to lying I felt I had no choice as I didn't want Mrs Grafton to know I was going out.

But I wasn't to get away so lightly. 'You are dressed up,' she said, looking me up and down suspiciously.

'I thought to walk to the village this morning for a breath of air,' I lied admirably.

'Well, be back in time, the Mistress demands punctuality,' the housekeeper warned me.

It was nearly nine, I managed to escape from Mrs Grafton, but felt she was suspicious of my intentions. Quickly I slipped out of the servants' entrance and walked across the front of the house and on to the short drive. Glancing back at the house I could see someone watching me from a side window of the main door. I was sure it was Mrs Grafton, this caused me to quicken my steps for I would not be thwarted.

Hastily, I undid the gate and closed it behind me, the latch clanging as I secured it. Thomas was waiting in the pony and trap, I ran to him and instructed him to move off quickly as I'd been seen.

'Calm yourself, pretty lady,' he said urging the pony forward, 'it will be all right.' He tried to reassure me, but it was futile. I knew what I was doing was underhanded and I knew that without a doubt I would be dismissed from my position. But if this were the case I may as well enjoy the day.

I really didn't know what had happened to me, but if it were love then it had certainly caused me to behave out of character.

The pony and trap bowled along through the village of Beckmoor, and as we passed Clara's cottage I thought that I had quite forgotten to speak with Antony Kershaw about her attending Emily's party. So taken was I with my desire to be with Thomas all other thoughts had flown from my head.

'A penny for your thoughts, sweetheart,' said Thomas clasping one of my hands in his.

'I've done a silly thing,' I answered him.

'And what would that be other than falling in love with me?' he teased. Could he never be serious, and strangely I felt quite irritated.

'I invited Clara White, Gladys' sister, to Emily's party next Thursday and I realised I had no right to do such a thing.' These words caused Thomas to pull the pony to a halt.

'Gladys White's sister at the Hall?' He mocked, 'Aunt Henry will never stand for it, you little fool.'

'How dare you call me a fool!' I lashed back at him, quite incensed. 'Your aunt may not like the idea, but Emily's father might. I have yet to broach the matter with him.'

'I wish you luck.' Thomas chuckled, urging the pony forward once more.

'Please take me back,' I said so suddenly I quite surprised myself. I had at last come to my senses, realising how wrong this was.

'I'm not turning back now, we are only two miles away and my mother is expecting us,' he said quite seriously for once.

'Your mother?' I exclaimed. 'You didn't mention your mother.'

'I surely didn't need to. Come on Abigail, smile and enjoy the day,' he coaxed.

There was nothing I could do, it were as if I were on a slippery path and couldn't get off. We travelled in silence for quite a while until Thomas pointed out the sea to our right. It shimmered calmly in the sunlight in total contrast to the never ending moorland.

Without warning Thomas pulled up outside a wooden gate and over the privet hedge I could see a delightful pink thatched cottage, an arch of white roses around the door, quite idyllic and picturesque.

'Welcome to Tidwell House,' he said.

'So this is your home,' I answered him, 'it is delightful.' And as I spoke I could see a middle-aged woman walking down the path to greet us.

Thomas chivalrously helped me alight from the trap and then introduced me to his smiling mother.

She was a nice looking woman for her age, a pleasant rounded face, greying hair secured at the nape of her neck with a plumpish figure dressed in an expensive blue gown with ruffles at her neck and sleeves.

We sat under a parasol in the splendid colourful garden, sipping cool lemonade and eating small sponge cakes. It was all very civilised, but somehow unreality set in, so I was startled when Mrs Craddock spoke. 'And what do you make of my sister?' she asked, looking directly at me intent on an answer.

'In truth, I've not seen much of her since my arrival,' I replied, unable to tell this sister of Henrietta's my true feelings.

'She has never been the same since her accident in the carriage thirty-five years ago.' Mary Craddock spoke almost as if relating a much told story. 'She will carry the scars to her grave, it has also scarred her personality. As a young woman she was kind and gentle, but now . . . ' Here she stopped.

'Please don't distress yourself,' I said kindly, for I could see the sadness on the woman's face.

'No I mustn't, for it was all so long ago and nothing can be altered,' she agreed. 'Now, I heard that you'd like to see Whitby.'

'Yes I would, and I need a haberdashery shop where I can purchase some silk flowers.' I told her.

'No need to find a shop, I have plenty in my sewing room, all different colours and sizes. Please come with me, Abigail.'

So we left Thomas alone in the garden and I stepped into the cottage with his mother. It was cool inside for which I was thankful. In the narrow hallway a picture of Kerslake Hall hung on the wall, no doubt a copy of the one that I had seen in the long gallery. It seemed that anyone with association to the Hall could not escape it and I wondered if I ever would, for the place had got under my skin and I already felt part of it.

Mrs Craddock led me up red thickly carpeted stairs, the place was cosy and inviting, unlike the Hall. She led me into a room which was full of sunlight. There were two tailor's dummies in the middle of the room, one of which held an unfinished yellow gown.

I was led to a large red pot in a corner which stood on a round table.

Inside were indeed many silk flowers of different colours and sizes.

'Pick out what you'd like, dear, for I have no use for all of them. I bought them because it is fashionable at the moment to decorate gowns with flowers. I gather this is what you want them for?' Mary Craddock enquired.

'Yes it is indeed, I wish to decorate my best blue dress in preparation for Emily's party next week,' I explained.

'That lovely child will be ten years old, I can hardly believe it. It is so sad about her poor mother. Now, you select your flowers while I go down and keep Thomas company. You will know your way?' she asked me.

'Yes, and thank you, Mrs Craddock.' I said politely, for it was indeed fortuitous.

I looked through the many silk flowers thinking of Alice's words that cream would be nice, but I'd spotted some small pale-pink-coloured ones which I felt sure would enhance the blue of the dress.

I picked out a dozen of them and then selected a large one identical in colour for my hair. I was about to turn away when on impulse I selected a large white one for Clara's dark hair, which brought to mind that I needed to speak urgently to Antony Kershaw.

Placing the flowers in my reticule I made my way back down the stairs, peeping into the open door of what was obviously the living room. It was very homely with matching floral curtains and chair covers.

Making my way back outside and through the garden, I marvelled at the beautiful colours of the flowers and how tall the mauve lupins were in all their splendour.

As I neared the table I could hear Mary Craddock's voice, 'Why do you have to associate with these young girls and women who have no direction in life and very little if not no means to support themselves? It really is beyond me, Thomas. She's a nice enough young woman and very nice looking, but then so is Barbara Middleton and she would marry you tomorrow! Her parents are wealthy and it would be more in keeping. I really don't understand you.' Here she stopped and I listened with baited breath for her son's reply.

'They are a challenge, Mother, that is all, I have no intention of marrying any of them. So let that reassure you.' As he spoke I saw him reach across and lay his hand across his mother's.

I was incensed. So, I was just a challenge was I? And who else had been such to him? Annie and Gladys were brought to mind. Oh no! How could I have been so naïve as to have fallen for this young man's charms? So far as to think that I was in love with him when all I appeared to be was a dalliance. I pulled myself together and made my way across to where they were sat.

'Here is Abigail,' declared Mrs Craddock, 'did you find what you needed dear?'

'Yes, thank you so much,' I said

sweetly, smiling at the both of them and in my heart wishing that Thomas were anywhere but in my presence. What a charmer he was, he'd certainly deceived me and I could never forgive him for making me look so foolish.

'Are you ready to go into Whitby?' Thomas asked me.

'Why yes, I think I am,' I answered, for a while here I thought I may as well see the town and I knew that I would not return in time to Kerslake Hall to read to my employer. What consequence this would have I had no idea but would soon find out.

The road to Whitby was not long and I could very soon see the ruined abbey high on the hill and smell the salt water and seaweed in the delightful harbour.

I managed to purchase myself a pretty turquoise sunshade with a few coppers I had in my reticule. All in all it was a pleasant afternoon and I endeavoured successfully to keep Mr Thomas Craddock at a distance much to his annoyance.

On our way back to the Hall I looked at the ruins of Whitby Abbey and thought that the abbey near Kerslake Hall would never hold such a joy for me after what I'd discovered today. We were silent all the way back and I was sure that Thomas was aware that something was amiss.

As we pulled up at the gates of the Hall Thomas bent across to me, his intention was to kiss me but I moved away from him.

'You may as well drive us to the main door,' I told him, 'for we are both in trouble anyway, me more so than yourself, your dear aunt will probably dismiss me as soon as she lays eyes on me,' I continued.

'I don't know what has changed you today, Abbey, but I am obviously wasting my time, at least if you are dismissed we won't have to see each other again.'

After this little speech he smiled at me and jumped down to open the gates. The cheek of the man I thought, and what could be gained by berating him; and I wondered for the second time that day how I could have been so foolish as to fall for such a cad as him.

As we pulled up outside the main door I knew that someone was sure to see us and when Mrs Grafton looked out of the downstairs window I knew my fate was sealed. I got down without assistance, my feet crunching on the gravel. I threw a look of disdain back at my companion and headed for the servants' entrance with Thomas's words ringing in my ears.

It was nearly six o'clock so I made my way to the kitchen, thankfully encountering no-one on the way. As I seated myself by Maggie she whispered, 'There's been a right carry on about you today, Miss,' she said.

'Has there indeed,' I answered quietly, 'in what way?'

'Mrs Grafton has been asking us all if we knew where you'd gone, but I didn't let on Miss, honest. And apparently the Mistress is right put out.' At these words her voice got louder and all at the table looked at me. What they were thinking I could not imagine.

Supper over, I made my way to my room hoping I would bump into Antony Kershaw to enable me to speak of Clara, but I encountered no-one, not even the hateful Mrs Grafton. I was quite surprised at this as on other occasions she had been ready to pounce on me at the time of my wrong doings and today's outing had surely beaten them all.

Stepping into my room I removed my bonnet and then tipped the silk flowers out of my reticule on to the bed. I went across to the wardrobe, took out the blue cotton dress and laid it on the bed too.

I glanced out of the window towards the brooding lake, my thoughts with Phoebe, Annie and Gladys, wondering as Alice had done who would be next.

The lake lay calm and still in the evening sunlight as if it held no secrets, almost innocent to the fact as to what had happened in its depths.

So engrossed was I in my thoughts that the sound of a key turning in the lock of my door didn't at first register itself in my head. As I laid the pink flowers on my blue dress thinking how becoming they were, I suddenly realised what I had heard but hardly given it any thought.

I went across to the door and turned the knob, pulling the door as hard as I could but it wouldn't budge. The awful truth dawned on me that I had been locked in and was a prisoner in my own bedroom.

7

It must have been Mrs Grafton I thought, the cunning woman that she was. On her mistress's instructions she had no doubt waited for me to return to my room after supper and turned the key in the lock, probably with jubilation that I had got my come-uppance.

I paced up and down, then tried to open the door again in the event that I had made a mistake. But to no avail, the door was locked fast. My only hope was Alice, I pounded my hands against the door as hard as I could, hurting my knuckles in the process but there was no response.

After a while I gave up and looked out of the window, watching as the sun fell farther in the sky, casting a pink glow on the still lake.

Even as I looked I could see a man walking on the path, I could tell by his clothes that it was Thomas which brought to mind the day's events. What a horrid day this had been and it was by no means over yet.

I saw Thomas step into the summer pavilion and then I lost sight of him. Had he a tryst with someone I wondered and certainly wouldn't put it past him. The sight of him had renewed my vigour and I proceeded to pound on the door again, but no-one heard me. Where was Alice?

My knuckles felt bruised now and I had to give up, hopefully someone would miss me in the morning. At the thought of all those hours spent in my room I felt utter despair and with my back against the door I slid on to the floorboards leaning wearily against the wood.

It seemed an eternity before I heard light footsteps in the corridor coming in my direction. I found some strength and got to my feet hammering on the door with one hand and at the same time shouting for help.

'Is that you, Miss Sinclair?' It was Maggie, I'd never before in my life been so pleased to hear another being's voice.

'Maggie, please help me, someone has locked the door of my room.' I spoke trying to keep my voice as calm as possible.

'Someone locked you in!' she exclaimed, 'I can hardly believe anyone could be so wicked.'

'Maggie, I want you to fetch Mr Kershaw, he's the only one that can get me out of here,' I said, knowing that Henrietta and her minion would not help me as I was sure they were the perpetrators of this injustice.

'But Mr Kershaw is drinking his port, Miss. I dare not disturb him,' she said with some reluctance.

'Maggie, you have to fetch him.' I said firmly or I'll be locked in here all night.

'I may lose my job, but all right, Miss, I'll go,' she agreed.

It seemed an eternity before I heard

footsteps again along the corridor. It was a man's tread, and to prove it Antony Kershaw's voice came to me through the door. 'Miss Sinclair, what is going on?'

'Someone has locked me in Sir, please get me out of here,' I pleaded with anger.

'Maggie, fetch Mrs Grafton please, now.' His voice was more authoritative than I had heard it before.

'Thank you, Mr Kershaw,' I said with relief. It wasn't very long before I heard Mrs Grafton's voice and then Mr Kershaw's.

'Open this door, Mrs Grafton.'

She obviously did as she was bid for I heard the jangle of her keys and the key turning in the lock. When the door opened the three of them stood there like characters in a painting, Maggie looking at me with dismay written all over her lovely face, Mrs Grafton with a sheepish look on hers and Antony Kershaw with a face like thunder, his blue eyes flashing with anger as he looked at Mrs Grafton.

'Did you do this, Mrs Grafton?' he shouted at her, 'for you are the only one with the means to do such a thing.'

'I did, Sir,' said the housekeeper calmly, 'on your mother's instructions.'

Maggie clapped her hands to her mouth, her eyes like saucers once more, looking at us all in disbelief.

'Go back to the kitchen, Maggie please,' said Antony Kershaw gently, 'none of this is your fault, indeed I thank you for fetching me.' At his words Maggie did as she was bid, but not before she'd dropped a brief curtsey to her master.

'Mrs Grafton, this is not the way I wish my household to be run,' he admonished her. 'You have given loyal service for many years, but I didn't expect your loyalty to my mother to extend to this.'

'And where is your mother?' I said speaking for the first time, 'for I wish to speak to her, no, I intend to speak to her.'

'Miss Sinclair,' Antony Kershaw said turning to me, 'I know how vexed you must be, but not tonight please.'

'Vexed!' I shouted the word, 'I am seething with anger and can no longer contain it.' So saying I pushed past them both and picking up my skirts headed for the stone staircase, both the Master and the housekeeper not far behind me.

'Miss Sinclair,' Mr Kershaw's voice shouted after me, but to no avail I moved faster and burst without ceremony into his mother's sitting room. The room was quite dark with only an oil lamp burning by her chair. Thankfully I could at least see her.

'What is this Miss Sinclair?' she shouted at me quite startled sitting up straighter in her chair.

'How dare you lock me in my room like some naughty child,' I screamed at her, 'I'm twenty-five years of age and have done nothing to you. Yet since I arrived here you seem intent on disliking me.'

'You went against my wishes and spent the day with my nephew,' she said quietly.

'Well I can assure you I shan't be spending time with him in the future, for he is nothing but a charming philanderer,' I said quite truthfully.

'I'll thank you not to speak like that about Thomas,' Henrietta said harshly, 'I will not have it.'

'Well, before you dismiss me, Miss Henrietta Kershaw, I resign, for to stay in this house any longer would be torture,' I said with triumph, pleased that I had at last answered her back.

'And where were you today, Miss Sinclair at two o'clock when I requested that you read to me? For after all that is what I employed you for.' Mrs Kershaw's words were true and she spoke them in a much softer tone.

'For that, I apologise,' I conceded, 'for I shouldn't have gone with Thomas, but unfortunately I let my heart rule my head.'

'Quite out of character I should

imagine Abigail, but I accept your apology, you have spirit and I like a girl with spirit.' I could not believe that Henrietta Kershaw had spoken these words.

'Please stay, Miss Sinclair,' Antony Kershaw's voice cut across our conversation. 'Don't be hasty,' he implored. I turned to look at him and saw Mrs Grafton hovering in the doorway.

'I'm tired now,' said the old lady, 'please leave me for I need to go to my bed. Sleep on it, girl,' she directed at me, 'and we shall continue this conversation another time.'

'Very well,' I agreed and bade her goodnight. Mrs Grafton stayed with her mistress while Antony Kershaw and I walked together along the corridor.

'Please accompany me to the drawing room, Miss Sinclair, for I wish to talk to you,' he requested. So I followed him and entered one of the hallowed rooms of Kerslake Hall.

'Would you like a glass of sherry to calm your nerves, Miss Sinclair, or perhaps a strong cup of sweet tea,' he asked.

'Tea sounds wonderful.' As I spoke he pulled a cord by the fireplace and in no time at all Maggie appeared, her expression agog as to what was going on.

'Miss Sinclair,' the master began, 'please think carefully about leaving for I would like you to stay. I know Emily has taken to you and please at least remain for her birthday party, for she has told me of her invitation to you.'

'Mr Kershaw, I have something to discuss with you concerning Emily's party.' I spoke realising that this was my chance to mention Clara. 'I did a very foolish thing the other day and invited Clara White to the party. It was something I did on impulse and I know it was wrong, but I feel it would be good for Emily to have another child to talk to.'

I said the words without taking a breath and waited for his reply. There was a long pause before he spoke.

'Then let her come, Miss Sinclair. That is if Clara's parents will agree to it.'

'Thank you, Mr Kershaw, I shall call and see Mr and Mrs White on Monday,' I said, relieved that the subject had been received so well.

'You do know, don't you, that Clara's sister was found in our lake?' he asked me.

'I do indeed. Are the police any nearer to solving the mystery?' I bravely said for really it was none of my business.

'Unfortunately not, but they do think someone held her underwater as bruises have been discovered on her neck,' he told me quite candidly, placing his cup and saucer back on the tray.

This piece of news alarmed me but I wouldn't let it show.

'Would you like to be moved to another room?' he said suddenly changing the conversation.

I was tempted to agree to this in view of the nocturnal occurrences, but quite surprised myself when I replied, 'No thank you, it is very kind of you, but I have settled in and am quite happy.'

'As long as you are sure,' he replied, 'for I wish you to be happy here, Miss Sinclair. I value your presence in the house and as for my cousin Thomas, he won't be here much longer to cause you distraction.'

'I feel very foolish regarding my association with your cousin,' I admitted.

'Let it not trouble you, Miss Sinclair, for he has many strings to his bow and is indeed charming to all the women folk he meets. I'm only sorry that he cast his spell on you, but please think no more of it. Look upon it as another lesson learned in the pursuit of love.'

His words were kind and understanding, but he had more to say. 'You no doubt know what happened to my wife, Phoebe, for it is difficult to keep anything secret in this household.'

'Yes, I did hear of her tragic accident

in the lake for which I am truly sorry.' I assured him.

'And it was an accident, although the residents of Beckmoor would have it that I killed her. To what gain I cannot imagine for all I have is a motherless child, a sad heart and this huge lonely house. Plus my mother who is not the easiest of people to please.'

He rambled on and I had half a mind to tell him of the incidents I'd experienced in the tower but no, I'd leave it until I got to know him better for it may only add to his distress. He continued, 'And there again I think the villagers confuse me for my cousin who cannot keep away from any pretty lass, young, old, rich or poor but I am not a philanderer, Miss Sinclair, no matter what accusations you may hear about me they are most probably untrue, I trust you believe me?'

'I do indeed,' I said honestly for I truly believed he was a good man.

'Then away to your bed young woman, you must be tired and accept my assurance that the unfortunate incident of this evening will not be repeated,' he said with sincerity.

'Thank you, Mr Kershaw,' I said rising from the comfortable chair, 'I'll bid you goodnight.'

As I reached the door his voice stopped me in my tracks. 'You look quite lovely when you are angry. Sleep well, Miss Sinclair.' I looked back at him and we smiled at each other. I felt at that moment we had forged a bond and I was thankful for it.

★   ★   ★

Reaching my room I felt quite elated, my blue dress still lay across the bed, the silk flowers strewn across it, all I had to do now was stitch them in place and look my best. But for whom? Certainly not Thomas Craddock and what about the master?

I felt now that I knew him better and quite warmed to him, but I must not be too hasty with my affections or see into things which did not exist.

As Antony Kershaw so rightly said, Thomas was a lesson in my pursuit of love. How astute he had been and not at all judgmental.

Snuggling down in the covers I went to sleep quite quickly only to be awoken a short time later by the piercing scream. I sat up in bed debating whether to go to the tower, but I decided against it as I was too weary, another night would have to suffice when I could unlock the mystery of the woman in white and I prayed also that the mystery surrounding Annie and Gladys's death would be resolved soon.

With these thoughts I drifted into a peaceful sleep, Antony Kershaw's words running through my mind. 'You look quite lovely when you are angry.' I smiled contentedly, not a thought of Thomas in my head.

★ ★ ★

Next day, I spent all afternoon stitching the flowers on the shoulders and waist of my blue dress. It was a painstaking task but the end result was worth it.

When I finished I hung the dress on the outside of the wardrobe so that any creases would have a chance to fall out. While sewing I thought how quickly my first week at the Hall had passed and of the many things that had happened since my arrival. The mystery woman in the tower, the demise of poor Gladys, teaching in the schoolroom and my unfortunate association with Thomas Craddock.

In view of what I'd learned of him the thought crossed my mind that he could after all be the man the police were searching for, but I dismissed the thought quickly from my mind, after all who was I to judge anyone?

'What have you been doing today, Miss?' asked Maggie at supper. On telling her of my dress for Emily's party she was keen to see it, 'Will you show me tomorrow afternoon please Miss as

116

it's my day off?' she asked with some excitement in her voice as I'd built up quite a rapport with Maggie.

'But of course. I have to go to the village in the morning, but I shall seek you out on my return.' Maggie seemed more than pleased about this.

That night all was quiet in the tower and I enjoyed an uninterrupted sleep. The next morning looking out of the window I could see that the good weather was still with us. I was a little apprehensive about calling at the Whites' cottage, but none-the-less felt I must go as I didn't wish to let anyone else down and Clara was probably looking forward to attending a party.

I decided to walk to the village and so set off after breakfast, no-one else was in sight on the road which cut its way through the moorland to the village. The cottage door was answered by Mrs White who stepped to one side so I could cross the brass doorstep.

'You've come to ask about Clara,' she said as I followed her into the small

117

kitchen-cum-living-room.

'I promised I would, Mrs White,' I said, 'how are you today?'

'I'm beginning to feel better.' As she spoke the words I could see that her cheeks looked pinker today replacing the pallor of last week.

'And have you reached a decision about Clara coming to the Hall with me on Thursday?' I asked gently, noting the bed made up under the large scrubbed table in one corner.

'Ay, we have,' said Mrs White, sitting on a kitchen chair by the table. 'Took my husband some persuading I can tell you, but Clara can come on the understanding that you won't let the child out of your sight.'

'That's splendid,' I enthused, 'and I give you my promise that I shall keep Clara safely with me. I'll collect her after school if that's all right with you.'

'Aye, and I trust you'll see her safely home.' Mrs White got up as she spoke and picked a package up off the small dresser. 'This is Clara's best dress, she has no other shoes, I'm afraid,' she said, handing me the brown paper package tied neatly with string.

'Don't worry, I will ensure she looks her best and I shall see Clara home myself,' I promised.

★   ★   ★

When I left the cottage some time later with the brown parcel under my arm, I bumped into Harry.

'How you doing, Miss?' he asked cheekily.

'Fine, thank you, Harry, everything is going splendidly.' Little did I know at that moment that things weren't as splendid as I thought.

Arriving back at the Hall I made my way to the kitchen to look for Maggie. She was sat at the table helping another maid to clean the silver which was spread out on a white sheet.

'Right, Miss, I'm coming,' said Maggie when she saw me. We walked up the stone staircase which was now so familiar to me. Maggie followed me into my room. I placed the parcel Mrs White had given me on the bed and then looked in dismay at my dress which still hung on the wardrobe. The flowers which I'd so carefully stitched on the day before were strewn on the floor. Some cruel person had systematically cut them away from the dress while I'd been out and my mind flew to Mrs Grafton.

8

Oh, Miss!' said Maggie helping me gather up the flowers. 'Who would do such a thing?'

'At this moment in time I have no idea, but intend to find out,' I said, placing the flowers on the bed once more.

'I'll help sew them back on Miss, I'm really quite good at needlework. I'd like to have done it for a living, but Ma says it would spoil my eyesight.' As she spoke I took down the dress and looked at it carefully, there were a couple of nicks in the fabric on the shoulder but this could be put right.

'Thank you for the offer Maggie, could we do it in your room?' I asked, not wanting to leave the dress here again for the same fate to befall it.

'We could Miss, I share the room with Ruth but she won't mind.'

* * *

We stitched together all evening, Maggie working on the waist and I on the shoulder, she was indeed a good needlewoman. From time to time I glanced around the room, almost taken up completely by two beds. I thought my room was sparse, but in comparison mine was a palace. There was just a rail placed in an alcove for their clothes which were few, and an old wooden stand on which stood a cracked washbowl and jug.

'There, that looks a picture, Miss,' said Maggie when we'd finished and I had to agree. 'I'll put it on the rail, Miss, and no-one but Ruth will see it.' So I entrusted my dress to Maggie's safe-keeping.

Thursday, the day of Emily's party arrived. It was the day I was asked for the first time to read to Mrs Kershaw. Today of all days when I had much to do, but after all, this is why I was here and until now my duties as companion had not been called upon except for that fateful day.

As I crossed the hall on my way to Mrs Kershaw's room I encountered Thomas, at the sight of him my heart missed a beat.

'Abbey,' he said quietly coming across to me, 'I need to speak to you about the other day. It was my misfortune . . . ' Here I interrupted him.

'No, Mr Craddock, it is my misfortune that I risked all for someone so indifferent to my feelings as yourself. Now if you'll please excuse me, Sir, I have to read to your aunt. I don't wish to give her any more cause to dismiss me.'

After this little speech I made to go but Thomas gently caught my arm. 'But I need to explain to you about the other day,' he implored.

'I fear there is nothing to explain,' I told him, wondering as I walked down the corridor what it was he had to say, just maybe I should have listened.

The consequence of my meeting with Thomas caused me distraction while reading to the old lady who was very subdued today. What was it Thomas wanted to explain? He called me a fool and suggested to his mother that I was a challenge. How could he possibly explain that. For the rest of the afternoon I turned it over and over in my mind wishing that I had at least listened to what he had to say.

* * *

After leaving Mrs Kershaw, I hurried up to my room as I still hadn't unpacked the parcel containing Clara's dress. Hurriedly I opened it, shook the dress and hung it up. It was blue quite similar in colour to mine with a wide bow at the back.

I knew that Clara would look charming and that we would compliment each other perfectly. I hastened along the road to Beckmoor fearing that I would be late, but as I reached the church door, Clara was just coming out.

'Hello, Clara, are you looking forward to the party?' I said trying to put her at ease.

'Yes, Miss, I've never been to a party before,' she replied softly and I could see she was nervous.

'I wish to see Miss Anderson,' I told Clara, steering her back through the door and instructing her to sit in a pew and wait for me. I climbed the stairs to the schoolroom, but the greeting died on my lips, for Ann Anderson and Antony Kershaw were in a close embrace. I retraced my steps down the stairs and taking Clara's hand we walked back out into the sunlight.

On reaching Kerslake Hall, I made my way with Clara to my room. First of all I would get Clara dressed and arrange her hair. As I slipped the dress over her head I thought how pretty she was. I sat her at the dressing table and brushed her hair until it shone and then placed the white flower in her hair. The finished result was wonderful. Maggie brought my dress to me and stayed to assist me.

'Can I do your hair please, Miss?' she asked of me.

'Of course,' I agreed and sat at the dressing table while Maggie brushed my long blonde locks and then twisted them at the back, securing it at the nape of my neck with pins, a tendril of hair each side of my face. All that remained was to position the pink flower. Maggie had done an admirable job.

'Stand up, Miss, and let's have a look at you,' she urged, excitedly. I did as I was bid. 'You look fit for a king, doesn't she, Clara?' Clara was sat quietly on the bed waiting patiently for me to prepare myself.

Suddenly there was a knock on the door, perhaps it was Alice, but on opening the door I was surprised to see Thomas standing in the doorway. 'I need to talk to you,' he said, heedless of Maggie and Clara.

'Tomorrow, Mr Craddock,' I promised, 'for you can surely see I have other things to do.'

'Tomorrow then,' he agreed, 'my mother is here by the way, and I have spoken to her. I'll see you in the dining-room.' So saying he left us, with me curious at to what he'd spoken to his mother about.

'Handsome gentleman, Miss,' Maggie cut into my thoughts.

'Yes, indeed he is. Thank you for helping me, if you could just show me to the dining-room now, please.'

I entered the dining-room with Clara clutching my hand. It was Emily dressed in a lemon dress who saw us first and came running over to us. 'Come and see the table,' she said to Clara, taking her hand.

I could see Henrietta Kershaw dressed in a pretty emerald green gown with lace at her throat. It was the first time I had seen her out of her sitting-room. Mary Craddock was talking to her sister, they both looked up,

Mrs Craddock smiling and indicating for me to join them.

It was then I spied Anthony Kershaw in deep conversation with the lovely Alice, who looked a picture in a violet-coloured silk gown. Neither of them noticed my arrival, but Thomas did and he came over to me.

'Sit here Miss Sinclair while I get you a sherry.' As he spoke, out of the corner of my eye I could see Henrietta Kershaw watching us. While Thomas went to get me a drink I sat at a table that was laden with small triangular sandwiches, jellies and iced sponge cakes, there was also a pink cake with candles on.

'Emily,' I called her over and she came running, Clara at her side, 'here is a small gift for your birthday from Clara and I.'

She took the small package from me and opened it.

'A lace handkerchief with my initial on it. Thank you, Miss Sinclair.' And she skipped over to her father, Clara following behind. At that moment Thomas returned with my drink which I sipped delicately not being used to partaking of sherry.

'Please meet me tomorrow morning in the rose garden at nine o'clock. Promise me, Abbey,' he whispered.

'I give you my promise,' I said, equally as quietly for Antony Kershaw and Alice were walking across to us.

Alice stood back quietly with that unfathomable expression. I wondered what she was thinking as she looked me up and down.

'I think it's time for tea,' said the master. I turned around to call Clara, but she'd disappeared and so had Emily, they'd obviously slipped out while the adults were talking.

'Oh, no,' I uttered, 'Where would they go? I promised Mrs White I'd keep her with me at all times.'

'Don't fret.' It was Thomas at my side. 'I will go and look for them, Miss Hayward, if you could try the nursery and Miss Sinclair and I will look outside,' he instructed.

'I'm concerned about the lake,' said Antony Kershaw, 'but I can't go out there.' So it was that Thomas and I walked around the lake together, it was still and serene in the evening sun.

'I can't wait until tomorrow,' he said, 'now is as good a time as any to explain myself.'

'It's not the right time, but I will hear you out,' I said, all the while scouring the paths of the lake.

'I hold in you high esteem, Abbey,' and he stopped walking. 'I didn't intend to call you a fool that day but the words slipped out without much thought to your reaction and I guess you heard Mother and I talking in the garden.'

'How do you know that?' I asked.

'Because of your change in manner, am I right?' His words were meant to be answered.

'Yes you are correct, I accidentally heard you tell your mother I was a challenge,' I said with some indignation. 'There they are!' I shouted as I saw the girls come out of the summer pavilion, each with a doll tucked under their arm. 'Emily, Clara,' I called to them, 'don't walk too close to the lake.' Then I addressed Thomas, 'We will continue this discussion in the morning if that meets with your approval.'

'It certainly does under the circumstances, and may I say, Abbey, that this evening, you look enchanting,' he complimented me.

When the girls reached us I hugged them both with relief, I held Clara's hand and Emily caught hold of her uncle's. We are like a young family I thought, out for a stroll in the evening sunshine and I knew beyond a doubt that deep in my heart this is what I longed for.

Thomas smiled at me, I'd like to have known what he was thinking. The remainder of Emily's party went well, the two children really had taken to each other and when Clara and I left, Emily spoke to her.

131

On delivering Clara safely back to the cottage I met Mr White. He was a sullen man, but thanked me and said how he never thought he would allow a child of his to visit Kerslake Hall.

'That's the one thing I can't understand about our Gladys,' he continued, 'she knew how I felt about it and ends up murdered in the Kershaw's lake.'

'I'm sure the police will find the truth,' I said, little knowing then that I would be the one to solve the mystery.

Next morning leaving my room to go down to breakfast, I glanced at the tower door and to my amazement realised it was open. I looked around me to see if anyone was about but all was silent in the corridor.

Quickly I made my way to the open door, looking up at the curved stairway I could sense no movement.

Bravely I walked up the stone staircase picking up my skirt as I went. I was nearly at the top step when I hesitated, what would I find? I was on the top step ready to step into the room beyond and when I did I gasped with surprise for the only thing the room held was a full-length mirror on a stand.

The rounded walls of the tower were of grey stone and I shivered at the thought of being locked in here. A candle-holder containing a half burnt candle stood solitary on the deep stone window ledge, a box of matches beside it.

Swiftly I made my way back down the stairs leaving the heavy wooden door ajar as I had found it. Mrs Grafton had said that it was unsafe to go in the tower, but I now knew this to be a lie. Why should she not want me to go up there when nothing of importance was there?

Looking at my fob watch I could see it was ten to eight and that I'd probably missed breakfast. Mrs Grafton came back to mind, was it her I mused, was she the night walker?

At exactly 9 o'clock I entered the rose garden, the sun still shone but surely this perfect weather couldn't hold out much longer I thought. Thomas was late.

Maybe he'd changed his mind, even as I thought it as if to prove me wrong, he stepped underneath the wooden rose arch and into the garden.

Quickly he came across to me and for some reason I glanced up at the window of the tower.

Someone was looking down at us and from this distance I was sure it was the housekeeper.

'Abbey, I'm sorry I'm a trifle late, please sit with me on this bench for I have much explaining to do,' he said, waiting for me to sit down. Then he sat next to me and again my heart skipped a beat. 'To call you a fool was very wrong of me, but I was so concerned as . . . ' Here he stopped.

'As what?' I coaxed him.

'I don't know if it's fair to tell you this, but I have suspicions about my cousin,' he admitted.

'Suspicions of what kind?' I asked.

'I'm unsure, Abbey. All I do know is that he has been seen with many of the young girls in the village and it is not for the want of romance. The subject is too delicate for your innocent ears. I was afraid that to bring Clara to the Hall would be foolish after her sister died here, but as it happened all went well and she is a charming child.'

'Then I forgive you, but I would like to say that I am not generally a foolish person,' I said, my head held high.

'And as for being a challenge, you are, but in the nicest possible way. My mother would have me marry Barbara Middleton, but it isn't what I need. Wealth and fine things are not for me. The scene I envisage is to love someone and to have that love returned, no matter what their position in life.

'Thank you for your explanation,' I said quietly, 'I am willing to accept it and forgive you.'

'Also I apologise for the compromising position I put you in the day you came to me in the long gallery, I could not help myself.' As he spoke I thought back to that day and could feel his hands stroking my hair.

'I'd quite forgotten that,' I lied.

'And one other thing,' said Thomas, drawing me to him, 'Will you make me the most fortunate of men and agree to marry me?'

9

This proposal quite surprised me and for some minutes I was lost for words, looking into Thomas' sparkling eyes I realised what a kind, endearing man he was and I truly believed he would be loyal. So much for Antony Kershaw's opinion that his cousin had many strings to his bow.

'Thomas,' I said quietly, taking hold of his hand. 'I am most flattered by your proposal, will you please give me time to think it over? And what would your mother say if we are to be married and where would we live?'

The questions tumbled from me one after another and Thomas placed his finger gently on my lips to silence me.

'So many questions, sweetheart. Fear not, for my mother will become used to the idea. After all she does like you and as to your question as to where we should live, at Tidwell if this would be suitable to you, for I love the place and cannot envisage living elsewhere.' Thomas squeezed my hand as he spoke.

'I would be happy to live at Tidwell, it is a beautiful dwelling, but will you wait a couple of days for my answer as this has come as a total surprise,' I pleaded.

'I shall wait with impatience and anticipation.' Thomas agreed.

We sat for some time talking and I mulled over whether to tell Thomas of the nighttime visitor to the tower. I made a sudden decision for with love must come trust.

'Thomas,' I proceeded to say, 'do you know who it is that visits the tower in the early hours?'

'The tower?' he said, obviously somewhat taken aback at the question, 'Why no, I don't. Come, tell me about it for I am a good listener.'

So I told him about the steps on the stairway, the piercing scream and the shuffling sounds, 'Also,' I continued, 'quite by chance I looked in the room of the tower and all that is in there is a mirror.'

'I'm quite at a loss,' said Thomas, 'but the mystery needs solving for it is obviously some unhappy soul. May I come to your room tonight and maybe we could go to the tower room together? For I cannot bear the thought of some harm befalling you and I promise,' here he laid his hand on his heart, 'my intentions are honourable.'

We both laughed at this and I felt again the way I did on my visit to Thurston Abbey, this seemed so long ago, but yet in truth it was little more than a week. As we parted Thomas gently brushed my lips with his own. The fleeting kiss was like a feather caressing my mouth, it stirred emotions in me that I had never before experienced and at our parting I felt cheated, of what I could only imagine.

★ ★ ★

That afternoon I read to Henrietta Kershaw again. Since the evening that I had been locked in my room the old lady had been sober towards me in manner and in voice even when she said, 'I'm told you are still dallying with my nephew.'

At these words I raised my eyes from the book I had been reading. 'You could do a lot worse and certainly no better than Thomas. What his mother will say if there is talk of marriage between you I dread to think. I'm not for it or against it, but you have spirit and the demeanour of a lady, and after all what is wealth? I have lived in this rambling house all my life and hardly stepped out of it, but it has brought me no joy. I wish you well, Abigail Sinclair.' Her words surprised me.

'Thank you.' I murmured and looking at her I felt compassion, after all it wasn't her fault that Antony's father had died. Also to have lived for years with a veil covering her face could not have been easy, especially when I recalled the portrait of her as a young woman in the long gallery.

As I opened the door of my bedroom I instinctively knew there was someone in the room. Cautiously I looked around the door and could see it was Alice. She was standing by the wardrobe, my blue dress over her arm.

'What are you doing?' I asked of her quite perplexed.

'I wanted to see how you'd stitched the flowers on,' she said quite calmly, 'and as you weren't about I didn't think you'd mind me taking a peek at it.'

'Well I do mind,' I answered, my brain working as I spoke, 'it was you wasn't it?' I said, realisation suddenly dawning on me.

'What do you mean?' she said, laying emphasis on the word *do*.

'I mean Alice, it was you who cut the flowers from my dress wasn't it?' I accused her, for I was sure I was correct in this assumption.

'Why on earth would I do such a thing?' she said innocently. This young woman was a very good liar.

'I have no idea why,' I said quietly, 'unless for some reason you are jealous of me.'

'And why would I be jealous of you?' she said with some sarcasm. 'Who would look twice at you in your dour grey dress?' At these words indignation rose in me.

'That is very unkind Alice, you may as well just own up to it for I know I am right.'

'You know nothing.' she said sharply, her temper was rising and I knew I must remain calm.

'What don't I know, Alice? Tell me, for unless I know I cannot help you.' My voice was level as I coaxed her for to shout now would achieve nothing. There was obviously some underlying problem with this woman, but I wasn't to be given the chance to find out.

'As if I'd tell you,' she retorted placing my dress back in the wardrobe. She then brushed past me to the open door and turned back to say, 'I wish you'd never come here.'

The words were spoken with such venom and ill feeling that I started trembling, unable to understand Alice's dislike of me for she had seemed so friendly when I first arrived at Kerslake Hall.

For some time I lay on my bed, the curtains drawn as I had a headache. Henrietta Kershaw's change of heart was on my mind, also Alice's sudden dislike of me. Or had it been sudden I asked myself, maybe on my arrival she had befriended me to gain knowledge of my intentions and I recalled her saying 'you'd not thought of marriage then?' At this thought I sat up, who did she think I might marry, Thomas or Antony?

Which brought to mind her admission, 'There is someone I truly love with all my heart.' Could it be Antony Kershaw or Thomas she was in love with? This caused me to think again of Thomas' proposal, he and his cousin had each accused the other of being a philanderer.

On the evening in the drawing-room I had been prepared to believe Antony Kershaw, now it seemed I believed Thomas, but who was right? I mulled it over for some time, it was little wonder I had a pounding head.

The fact that I'd seen Antony with Ann Anderson led me to believe he wasn't entirely honest, for had he not spoken sweet words to me? I'd made my decision, it was Thomas I believed, but I did not get chance to think of his proposal of marriage for I slipped into a peaceful slumber.

Sometime later I was awoken by someone tapping on my door. I sat up and looked around me, the sun had moved across the sky, I must have been asleep for some time.

'Who is it?' I called out, getting up and drawing back the curtains.

'It's me Miss,' said Maggie stepping into the room and closing the door behind her, 'I was right worried when you didn't appear at teatime, Miss.'

'Please call me Abbey,' I said to her.

'You look awful, Miss Abbey,' she said.

'Do I really?' I asked her with some dismay going to look in the mirror. My hair had partly escaped the pins and my face was white. I poured some cold water in the china bowl splashing my face with it and pinching my cheeks to bring back some colour to my skin, then I released my hair from the pins and started to brush it.

'I'll do that for you, Miss Abbey,' said Maggie.

'Thank you, but I'll leave it now, it's hardly worth rearranging it,' I said looking at the clock which showed it was nearly nine o'clock. I must have slept for hours and felt quite hungry.

As if by magic Maggie said, 'I brought you this from the kitchen, I put it in my pocket when Ada wasn't watching.' As she spoke Maggie produced some bread and cheese from her pocket.

I devoured it fairly quickly thanking her for thinking of me. What I really needed was a cup of hot tea, but eating had revived me and I was to be thankful to Maggie for little did I know then that it would be a long night.

'You could come down to the kitchen and I could make you some tea Miss Abbey, it's Cook's night off.' She said when I told her I needed a drink. So without thinking I followed her down to the kitchen, my long blonde hair falling in waves down my back. It was only when we encountered Mrs Grafton that I realised and suddenly felt very vulnerable in the housekeeper's presence.

'My mistress wishes to speak to you in her sitting room,' she said, 'I was on my way to fetch you. And what are you both doing skulking around the place at this time of night.' As she spoke she looked at Maggie.

'I'm going to make a pot of tea for us, Mrs Grafton.' Maggie said with spirit, almost defying the housekeeper to stop us.

'Then make it and get back to your

room. As for you, Miss Sinclair. It will not do for you to walk around the house with your hair flowing behind you.' As she walked away I almost giggled at her words. In fact Maggie and I did laugh like a couple of naughty children.

'Please make the tea, Maggie, while I go and see what Mrs Kershaw requires of me, and I'm sorry I was irritable just now but I had just woken up, forgive me?' I asked.

'Of course, Miss, I'll see you in the kitchen,' she said.

As I approached Henrietta's sitting-room I could hear raised voices, the door was slightly ajar and I heard Mrs Kershaw's voice.

'You will not marry her she is beneath you.' Holding my breath I waited to hear the reply.

Thankfully it was Antony and not Thomas who spoke, 'If I wish to marry Miss Anderson, you will not stop me. All my life you have domineered me and I have done your bidding, but over this I will not be moved,' he said emphatically.

'I forbid you to bring her to this house,' said Henrietta harshly.

'But it is my house, mother and I shall bring who I like here and that is my final word.'

As he spoke I scurried back along the corridor and joined Maggie in the kitchen for a cup of tea, all the while thinking that Henrietta Kershaw was losing her grip on this household, including the master, and he it would appear was to be married. Very obviously love was in the air.

Thomas kept to his word and came to my room at twelve-thirty that night. I'd had the foresight to tie back my hair with a blue ribbon. As I let him in he said, 'Fear not lovely lady for I come to your room with good intentions and only to assist you in solving the mystery of the tower,' and I laughed. The thought crossing my mind that he would make a good husband for he managed to cause merriment all the time.

At a quarter to one we sat together quietly on the bed waiting for the footsteps. No mention had been made of marriage and I felt quite despondent, then realised it wasn't really the right time to talk of such things. My thoughts were interrupted by the sound of footsteps. We both got to our feet and quickly made our way to the door of the tower being as quiet as possible.

Thomas held my hand, the corridor was silent and I fell a few steps behind him feeling quite nervous. The tower door was ajar and we gently eased it back so we could pass through.

The light of the candle from above lighting the stone steps before us. I lifted my skirts as I followed Thomas towards the curve in the stairway. It was then that the piercing scream came. Close to it was far worse than I'd heard it in my bedroom, I clapped my hands over my ears as I could hardly bear it.

When it stopped the sound of it still echoed faintly round the tower, Thomas moved forward and beckoned me on. We stood almost touching in the final step, with the woman in white before us her frame almost obscuring the narrow mirror.

Even as we looked she held the candle high and turned slowly around. I gasped when I saw the twisted face before us, it was then she saw us. I looked mesmerised by the pink scars on her cheeks and could see she only had one eye. I looked at the bright red rouge on the twisted mouth and knew without a doubt it was Henrietta Kershaw.

'So you've seen me now,' she said, a sob escaping her lips. 'Now what will you do, hate me more?' And the tears started to roll down her cheeks.

'We don't hate you, Aunt Henry,' said Thomas with compassion in his voice, and in that moment I was certain that I loved him.

'I've lived with this for thirty-five years. Some nights I just have to look at myself hoping that at some time I would find myself beautiful again, but I still see the same scars and my heart is heavy for I want the old me back.' As she spoke the candle wavered in her hand and Thomas gently took it from her and I could see that the old lady's hair was a beautiful silver grey falling over her shoulders. The more I looked at her the less I noticed her twisted face and could see the poor tormented soul that lay behind it.

'Come, Aunt Henry,' said Thomas gently, 'let me take you back to your room.'

'I will do that, Sir.' We turned around to see Mrs Grafton on the stairs, a candle in her hand and I could now understand her loyalty to the poor creature who stood in the tower.

'How did you know, Thomas?' His aunt asked of him.

'Abbey, I mean Miss Sinclair, has heard you most nights since her arrival,' he explained.

'And how is that, Abigail?' the old lady directed at me, but Mrs Grafton gave me no chance to answer.

'I put her in the room next to the tower, hoping she would succumb to it as the others before her and leave. I'm sorry, Mistress, but you don't need anyone else when you have me.'

'Jealousy is a terrible thing, Beatrice Grafton,' began Mrs Kershaw, then she turned her attention to me.

'Take heed of my words, Abigail, for they will stand you in good stead.' At her words my mind flew to Alice. Thomas took his aunt's hand and led her to Mrs Grafton.

Before they descended the stairs Henrietta Kershaw turned back and looking at me said, 'Value your beauty Abigail for one day it will be gone.' With those words Mrs Grafton took her mistress back to her room.

I wept and Thomas gently laid my head on his shoulder smoothing my hair. I could see our reflection in the mirror, we were united and I knew that I not only loved him, but was destined to be with him.

'Was it a shock for you also?' I asked

him when I'd calmed down.

'Indeed it was, for I had never seen her face, I shall speak to Antony later and suggest that this mirror be removed for the only purpose it is serving is to distress my aunt each time she comes up here,' he told me.

Later, back on my own in my room, I looked out of the window thinking of Henrietta, poor lady. The full moon glimmered on the lake almost dividing it in two. The beauty of it called me and against my better judgement I decided to walk around it and sit in the summer pavilion with my thoughts in the moonlight.

10

The servants' entrance was locked, but the key had been left in the door, I turned it gently although I knew that no-one was likely to be around at two-thirty in the morning. My only concern was that someone would lock the door again before I came back in, but I didn't intend to be long.

After the discovery Thomas and I had made in the tower I needed some fresh air before I tried to sleep. Thomas had gone back to the long gallery to finish some notes he was making.

Everything looked different at night and I could hear the hooting of an owl somewhere nearby on the moor. I could see the outline of the summer pavilion towards which I was heading. I stopped suddenly as I thought I heard another footstep on the path, but looking around I could see no-one was there. It had obviously been an echo of my own. I moved on marvelling at how the lake shimmered with white light, but in some parts seeming black and deep and mysterious.

I shivered, apprehension taking over me and I stopped again, uncertain of whether to go forward or to retrace my steps. I shivered again, but decided to proceed to the summer pavilion, for after all what harm could possibly befall me at this late hour.

A small area of grass surrounded the small building and I stepped noiselessly across the springy damp turf, my shoes feeling damp as I stepped on to what appeared to be a marble floor. In the centre of the floor was a small round table surrounded by four white intricately carved seats. I sat on one and realised it was made of some kind of heavy metal as it felt cold to the touch.

It was certainly a lovely spot as it commanded a view of the lake and the house which was outlined by the light of the moon. To look at Kerslake Hall from here on a quiet, warm, still early morning the building appeared tranquil and calm. I glanced at the tower and could hardly believe I had entered it with Thomas only a couple of hours before.

The whole episode now seeming unreal to me, I could heard the water lapping gently against the ground and shivered again as I thought of what had happened in its depths. Rising to my feet I moved out of the pavilion.

As I stepped on to the grass a figure loomed suddenly before me and my heart started racing, but I could see it was only Alice and my heartbeat steadied itself.

'What are you doing here?' I asked, my voice quivering, for although a warm night I suddenly felt very cold and wished I wore a shawl over my shoulders.

'I could ask you the same question.' Alice's voice was calm and as the moonlight fell on her face she looked almost ethereal as if she were made of alabaster.

'I couldn't sleep,' I explained, 'and the lake looked so beautiful tonight.'

'Yes,' Alice said dreamily, 'it is rather lovely. I couldn't sleep either and saw you from my window walking along the path so I thought to join you and apologise for my behaviour earlier.'

'Thank you for your apology,' I said, my voice quite steady now.

'Shall we walk together back to the house?' asked Alice in a quiet friendly manner.

'Yes,' I agreed.

'Please could you walk next to the lake as I hate the water and cannot swim,' she admitted.

'But of course. For even though I can't swim I have no fear of water.' Were the words I spoke true I wondered as I looked into the lake's murky depths.

We continued walking in what seemed like a companionable silence then the moon was hidden momentarily behind a cloud and I suddenly felt my whole body being pushed to the ground. Something caught my side and I suddenly realised we were at the spot where Phoebe had died and it was her plaque that had caused me such pain.

For seconds I couldn't imagine what had happened to me, then I felt Alice push me further to the ground and I realised with horror that my head was hanging over the lake. I could feel the cold water seeping through my hair. I looked up at her unable to comprehend fully what was happening.

'It's you!' I said foolishly. 'You who murdered Annie and Gladys, but for what reason, and now why me?' A sob escaped my lips and I felt Alice push my head under the water. She was strong but I was stronger, I fought against her hands and within seconds came out of the water, gasping and spluttering for air.

'No-one will have him but ME!' Alice screamed. She looked like a mad woman and all the beauty had gone out of her face.

'Who are you talking about?' I managed to gasp, my lungs near to bursting point.

'The master of course!' As she spoke I could feel her weight on my body. I just needed to take her off guard, get her to talk I thought to myself.

'But I have no interest in Antony Kershaw,' I said quietly, my strength suddenly returning.

'Don't lie!' she screamed, 'I heard you in the drawing-room together, he said you were lovely and he tried to gain an encounter with Annie and Gladys, I couldn't bear that so I lured them here on the pretence that they could be a maid here at the Hall.'

Her grip on me was relaxing. I took my chance and pushed her off me with all my strength and scrambled to my feet. My legs would hardly run although I made the effort but Alice ran faster and caught at my legs pulling me off my feet once more. As she went to hold me down I rolled over and the next thing I heard was a splash in the water, horrified I could see Alice thrashing about in the lake.

'Please help me,' she called, 'I can't swim, I shall drown.' I lay on the side of the lake and stretched out my arm to her, but she couldn't reach it. Try as I might to grasp her hand it was to no avail. 'It is deep,' were the last words I heard from her before the lake enveloped her whole body.

I heard someone running on the path, suddenly I looked up into Thomas's face and felt him gather me in his arms, when mercifully I slipped into unconsciousness. Maggie was the first person I saw on waking. She sat on a wooden chair, her anxious face looking down at me.

'Miss Abbey, you're awake,' she declared with obvious joy, 'you've slept for twenty-four hours, everyone is right concerned about you. I'll just tell someone you're awake.'

As Maggie left I struggled to sit up and realised I was in a large bed in unfamiliar surroundings. The horror of my tussle with Alice came back to me and I sank back again on the plump pillow. Oh Lord, I thought, I give thanks that I'm alive and what of Alice. This thought agitated me.

Maggie returned with Thomas, my beloved Thomas. He sat on the chair and reaching for my hand clasped it securely in his own.

'Sweetheart,' he said gently, 'can you recall what happened?'

'Only too well.' I answered with a voice that didn't seem my own. 'Is that rain?' I asked, for as I looked at the long window draped with red curtains I fancied I could hear rain splattering on the grass.

'Yes it is my love, but think not of the weather. Can you tell me what happened?' he asked stroking the back of my hand with his free one.

'How . . . how did you know that I was by the lake for it was you who came to me, wasn't it?' I stammered, the full picture coming back in my mind.

'I saw you walking with someone as I

161

looked from the long gallery window, you were quite clear in the moonlight, then as the cloud overshadowed the moon I lost sight of you briefly and when the light returned I could see you both on the ground. Fearing someone had fallen in the lake I hastened down to you, but it was too late to save Alice,' Thomas told me.

'Is she dead then?' I asked quietly.

'Yes I am afraid so.' He squeezed my hand as he told me.

'She tried to kill me,' I admitted, a sob escaping my lips. 'She held my head underwater. She also killed poor Annie and Gladys,' I told him, tears of relief streaming down my face.

'That explains why your lovely hair was wringing wet, I must tell my cousin who is with the police at this moment. We did think there was something strange about it all. What possessed you to walk out at such a time?' asked Thomas.

'It was the moonlight, everything looked so pleasant, I thought the fresh air would help me sleep, but the lake will now only hold dread for me whether by sunlight or the silvery light of the moon.' As I spoke I looked across Thomas' shoulder and gave an encouraging smile to Maggie who looked quite worried.

'Try to put it from your mind, Maggie will get you some hot broth while I speak to Antony.' As Thomas left me he gave my hand a loving squeeze, but I knew that no matter how hard I tried the thought of that night would take a long time to fade from my memory. I would keep feeling my head under water and see Alice thrashing about in the cool lake.

When I was strong enough I got out of bed and with Maggie's help went to look from the window, the sun was shining again and thankfully I was at the front of the building. I would have to leave this place as soon as I was able.

11

When that day arrived, I asked Maggie if she would kindly gather my things together in my valise for me, to which she agreed. I'd seen little of Thomas since the day I awoke, nothing had been said about his proposal of marriage and I was beginning to think I'd dreamt everything good and bad since I'd arrived at Kerslake Hall.

Maggie brought my packed valise to me, my best blue dress and petticoat over her arm.

'Two people have requested to see you,' she ordered, and so I did as I was bid, slipping the blue dress on and thinking of Alice as I did so, and how she'd cut off the silk flowers in a frenzy of jealousy.

'And who wishes to see me?' I asked Maggie, straightening the skirts of my dress and thinking how loose it was at the waist. I'd obviously lost weight, but who wouldn't after the ordeal I'd been through.

'Mrs Kershaw and Mr Craddock in that order, Miss Abbey,' Maggie told me as she brushed and arranged my hair on her insistence.

So I walked towards the main staircase at Kerslake Hall. As I reached the top of it I could see that I was on the opposite side of the long gallery. Seeing the door I went to open it and stepped inside looking at the paintings on the wall recalling how Thomas had loosened my hair that day which seemed so long ago.

I walked down to the portrait of Henrietta Kershaw and stood for some time looking at the lovely face which looked back at me and I thought of the old lady's words that night in the tower, 'Value your beauty Abigail, cherish it for one day it will be gone.'

As I made my way back to the door, I took a look through the squint in the wall and could see Thomas crossing the hall to what I now knew to be the drawing-room and in my mind could see Alice crossing the hall on that other occasion.

Alice, who had turned out to be a murderess. I shuddered at the very thought of myself lying under the still water of the lake and made my way back to the stairs, descending them slowly to the black and white hall below, the hem of my blue skirts brushing the carpet beneath my feet.

Tapping on Mrs Kershaw's sitting-room door, I recalled the day of my arrival and my employer's acid tongue. Since then in a few short weeks I had learnt much about her and could forgive her.

'Come in,' called a much softer voice. I opened the door and entered the room, sunlight did not flood the room with its rays at this time of day so I did not feel at a disadvantage as I had on that other occasion.

'You look well, Abigail. A little thinner it is true, but after all you have been through could any one of us be surprised.' As Henrietta Kershaw spoke I looked at her, gone was the veil and she wore a cheerful red dress which suited her silver grey hair.

Like anyone else I would see through the scars and twisted face to see the person beneath. The woman I now looked at was far different to the sharp, bitter old lady who had been there before. 'I thank you and my nephew,' she continued, 'for I have decided to make the most of my life and hide away no longer.'

'That is good to hear, Mrs Kershaw,' I said honestly.

'I understand you wish to leave us,' the new Henrietta observed.

'That is true, for after my experience at the lake,' here my voice trembled, 'I sadly cannot stay.'

'I shall be sorry to see you go,' said Henrietta, 'for you stood up to me and helped me to see myself as I had become over the years, but trust me when I say you have a good life ahead of you and you've not seen the last of me, I promise.'

What she meant by this I didn't know, but would no doubt find out soon. 'Thank you,' I said.

'Come closer to me for I have something for you,' said the old lady. I did as Henrietta bid and she handed me an emerald necklace and the box to go with it. 'I want you to have this, for it was my mother's.'

'But Mrs Kershaw,' I gasped, 'I cannot take something so precious from you.' As I spoke I looked at the sparkling gem at the end of a gold chain.

'I insist you have it, there is a reason, and this is my gift to you. Be happy, Abigail.' With these words I felt I was dismissed.

Walking along the corridor I placed the lovely necklace in its box. Maggie stood in the hall with my valise and some other luggage at her feet.

'But that isn't all mine,' I exclaimed.

'No Miss, it isn't, but that's not for

me to explain. Mr Craddock wishes to see you in the drawing-room.' Her voice was full of excitement and I was more than curious.

The drawing-room door was open, I pushed it wider still and could see Thomas standing by the fireplace, a bright sun streamed in and the room seemed so different from that evening when I had sat in here with Antony.

'You are better, sweetheart,' Thomas said, coming across to me and shutting the door. 'Can we now talk of love and marriage?' he asked, his blue eyes twinkling at me.

'Thomas I thought you'd changed your mind.'

'Never,' he replied, handing me a small box. 'Now, answer me, will you make me the most fortunate of men and agree to marry me?' he said solemnly.

'Yes, oh yes!' I said, looking at him as I spoke and all I wanted to do was fall into his strong arms and feel safe for always.

'Open it then,' he urged, looking at the small green box in my hand and I realised it matched the one I held which Henrietta had handed to me earlier. On opening it I could see it held an emerald ring which was surrounded by a circle of small sparkling diamonds.

'It is so beautiful, and matches the necklace your aunt has just given me,' I enthused. 'You are very obviously in collusion over this.'

'We are indeed,' he agreed, 'the ring and the necklace were my grandmother's.' As he spoke he placed the pretty ring on my finger and kissed it. 'So, our betrothal is sealed, and our love?' he questioned. My heart was racing but not with fear this time but untold happiness.

'Thank you so much, Thomas. I am the most fortunate of women.' And we laughed.

'One other thing, sweetheart. If it is favourable with you I am moving us to Tidwell today, along with Maggie, who implored that she be allowed to be your maid if you agreed to marry me.'

At his words I felt such happiness for I had become very fond of Maggie and to live in the peace and tranquillity of the cottage would be I was sure like residing in heaven.

The brougham was waiting outside for the three of us. Maggie was smiling as if she'd never stop, there was a spring in my step again and Thomas looked delighted.

As we drove out of the gates I looked back at Kerslake Hall and I knew I would never see the brooding lake again. But many times Emily would stay with us at Tidwell and Aunt Henrietta would visit, also Antony and Ann after their marriage.

As we stepped through the small wooden gate of Tidwell House, Mary Craddock stood under the roses at the doorway in greeting, while Maggie carried my small valise up the path. Thomas drew me to him. 'Welcome home Abbey, and I love you,' he said.

'I love you too,' I murmured as we walked up the path together hand in hand and I knew that our lives were just beginning.

THE END

We do hope that you have enjoyed reading this large print book.

Did you know that all of our titles are available for purchase?

We publish a wide range of high quality large print books including:
Romances, Mysteries, Classics
General Fiction
Non Fiction and Westerns

Special interest titles available in large print are:
The Little Oxford Dictionary
Music Book, Song Book
Hymn Book, Service Book

Also available from us courtesy of Oxford University Press:
Young Readers' Dictionary
(large print edition)
Young Readers' Thesaurus
(large print edition)

For further information or a free brochure, please contact us at:
Ulverscroft Large Print Books Ltd.,
The Green, Bradgate Road, Anstey,
Leicester, LE7 7FU, England.
Tel: (00 44) **0116 236 4325**
Fax: (00 44) **0116 234 0205**

Other titles in the
Linford Romance Library:

IN THE HEART OF LOVE

Judy Chard

Alison Ross's humdrum life is violently changed when kidnappers take her daughter, Susi, mistaking her for the granddaughter of business tycoon David Beresford, in whose offices Alison is employed. The kidnappers realise their mistake and Susi's life is in danger. Now Alison's peaceful existence in the Devon countryside becomes embroiled not only in horror, but also unexpected romance. But this is threatened by spiteful gossip concerning her innocent relationships with the two men who wish to marry her . . .

OUT OF THE SHADOWS

Catriona McCuaig

Newly single and enjoying her job as an office temp, Rowena Dexter sees new hope for the future when she starts dating barrister Tom Forrest. But memories of a terrifying childhood incident resurface when she receives threatening e-mails. She was in the house when her aunt was murdered, and the case has never been solved. Rowena's former husband, Bruce, agrees to help her unmask the stalker, but can they solve the mystery before the murderer strikes again?

CHATEAU OF THE WINDMILL

Sheila Benton

Hannah's employer, a public relations agency, has despatched her to France to handle the promotion of a Chateau which is to be converted to an hotel. However Gerrard, the son of the owner, resents the conversion, and some of the residents of the Chateau are not what they seem to be. Now she begins to find herself entangled both in a mystery that surrounds a valuable tapestry, and also a Frenchman's romantic intentions . . .